F. Anstey

The tinted Venus

A farcical Romance

F. Anstey

The tinted Venus
A farcical Romance

ISBN/EAN: 9783743332737

Manufactured in Europe, USA, Canada, Australia, Japa

Cover: Foto ©Andreas Hilbeck / pixelio.de

Manufactured and distributed by brebook publishing software
(www.brebook.com)

F. Anstey

The tinted Venus

CONTENTS.

LIST OF ILLUSTRATIONS.

I.

" Ther hopped Hawkyn,
Ther daunsed Dawkyn,
Ther trumped Tomkyn . . . "
The Tournament of Tottenham.

IN Southampton Row, Bloomsbury, there is a small alley or passage leading into Queen Square, and rendered inaccessible to all but foot passengers by some iron posts. The shops in this passage are of a subdued exterior, and are overshadowed by a dingy old edifice dedicated to St. George the Martyr, which seems to have begun its existence as a rather handsome chapel, and to have improved itself, by a sort of evolution, into a singularly ugly church.

Into this alley, one Saturday afternoon late in October, came a short stout young man, with sandy hair, and a perpetual grin denoting anticipation rather than enjoyment. Opposite the church he stopped at a hairdresser's shop, which bore the name of Tweddle. The display in the window was chastely severe; the conventional half-lady revolving slowly in fatuous self-satisfaction, and the gentleman bearing a piebald beard with waxen resignation, were not to be found in this shop-front, which exhibited nothing but a small pile of toilet remedies and a few lengths of hair of graduated tints. It was doubtful, perhaps, whether such self-restraint on the part of its proprietor was the result of a distaste for empty show, or a conviction that the neighbourhood did not expect it.

Inside the shop there was nobody but a small boy, corking and labelling bottles; but before he could answer any question as to the whereabouts of his employer, that artist made his appearance. Leander Tweddle was about thirty, of middle height, with a luxuriant head of brown hair, and carefully-trimmed whiskers that curled round towards his upper lip, where they spent themselves in a faint moustache. His eyes were rather small, and his nose had a decided upward tendency; but, with his pink-and-white complexion and compact well-made figure, he was far from ill-looking, though he thought himself even farther.

"Well, Jauncy," he said, after the first greetings, "so you haven't forgot our appointment?"

"Why, no," explained his friend; "but I never thought I should get away in time to keep it. We've been in court all the morning with motions and short causes, and the old Vice sat on till past three; and when we did get back to chambers, Splitter kep' me there discussing an opinion of his I couldn't agree with, and I was ever so long before I got him to alter it my way."

For he was clerk to a barrister in good practice, and it was Jauncy's pride to discover an occasional verbal slip in some of his employer's more hastily written opinions on cases, and suggest improvements.

"Well, James," said the hairdresser, "I don't know that I could have got away myself any earlier. I've been so absorbed in the laborrit'ry, what with three rejuvenators and an elixir all on the simmer together, I almost gave way under the strain of it; but they're set to cool now, and I'm ready to go as soon as you please."

6

"Now," said Jauncy, briskly, as they left the shop together, "if we're to get up to Rosherwich Gardens to-night, we mustn't dawdle."

"I just want to look in here a minute," said Tweddle, stopping before the window of a working-jeweller, who sat there in a narrow partition facing the light, with a great horn lens protruding from one of his eyes like a monstrous growth. "I left something there to be altered, and I may as well see if it's done."

Apparently it was done, for he came out almost immediately, thrusting a small cardboard box into his pocket as he rejoined his friend. "Now we'd better take a cab up to Fenchurch Street," said Jauncy. "Can't keep those girls standing about on the platform."

As they drove along, Tweddle observed, "I didn't understand that our party was to include the fair sect, James?"

"Didn't you? I thought my letter said so plain enough. I'm an engaged man now, you know, Tweddle. It wouldn't do if I went out to enjoy myself and left my young lady at home!"

"No," agreed Leander Tweddle, with a moral twinge, "no, James. I'd forgot you were engaged. What's the lady's name, by-the-by?"

"Parkinson ; Bella Parkinson," was the answer.

Leander had turned a deeper colour. "Did you say," he asked, looking out of the window on his side of the hansom, "that there was another lady going down?"

"Only Bella's sister, Ada. She's a regular jolly girl, Ada is, you'll—— Hullo!"

For Tweddle had suddenly thrust his stick up the trap and stopped the cab. "I'm very sorry, James," he said, preparing to get out, "but—but you'll have to excuse me being of your company."

7

"Do you mean that my Bella and her sister are not good enough company for you?" demanded Jauncy. "You were a shop-assistant yourself, Tweddle, only a short while ago!"

"I know that, James, I know; and it isn't that—far from it. I'm sure they are two as respectable girls, and quite the ladies in every respect, as I'd wish to meet. Only the fact is——"

The driver was listening through the trap, and before Leander would say more he told him to drive on till further orders, after which he continued—

"The fact is—we haven't met for so long that I dare say you're unaware of it—but *I'm* engaged, James, too!"

"Wish you joy with all my heart, Tweddle; but what then?"

"Why," exclaimed Leander, "my Matilda (that's *her* name) is the dearest girl, James; but she's most uncommon partickler, and I don't think she'd like my going to a place of open-air entertainment where there's dancing—and I'll get out here, please!"

"Gammon!" said Jauncy. "That isn't it, Tweddle; don't try and humbug me. You were ready enough to go just now. You've a better reason than that!"

"James, I'll tell you the truth; I have. In earlier days, James, I used constantly to be meeting Miss Parkinson and her sister in serciety, and I dare say I made myself so pleasant and agreeable (you know what a way that is of mine), that Miss Ada (not *your* lady, of course) may have thought I meant something special by it, and there's no saying but what it might have come in time to our keeping company, only I happened just then to see Matilda, and—and I haven't been near the Parkinsons ever since. So you can see for yourself that a meeting might be awkward for all parties concerned; and I really must get out, James!"

Jauncy forced him back. "It's all nonsense, Tweddle," he said, "you can't back out of it now! Don't make a fuss about nothing. Ada don't look as if she'd been breaking her heart for you!"

"You never can tell with women," said the hairdresser, sententiously; "and meeting me sudden, and learning it could never be—no one can say how she mightn't take it!"

"I call it too bad!" exclaimed Jauncy. "Here have I been counting on you to make the ladies enjoy themselves—for I haven't your gift of entertaining conversation, and don't pretend to it—and you go and leave me in the lurch, and spoil their evening for them!"

"If I thought I was doing that——" said Leander, hesitating.

"You are, you know you are!" persisted Jauncy, who was naturally anxious to avoid the reduction of his party to so inconvenient a number as three.

"And see here, Tweddle, you needn't say anything of your engagement unless you like. I give you my word I won't, not even to Bella, if you'll only come! As to Ada, she can take care of herself, unless I'm very much mistaken in her. So come along, like a good chap!"

"I give in, James; I give in," said Leander. "A promise is a promise, and yet I feel somehow I'm doing wrong to go, and as if no good would come of it. I do indeed!"

And so he did not stop the cab a second time, and allowed himself to be taken without further protest to Fenchurch Street Station, on the platform of which they found the Misses Parkinson waiting for them.

Miss Bella Parkinson, the elder of the two, who was

employed in a large toy and fancy goods establishment
in the neighbourhood of Westbourne Grove, was tall and
slim, with pale eyes and auburn hair. She had some
claims to good looks, in spite of a slightly pasty complexion, and a large and decidedly unamiable mouth.

Her sister Ada was the more pleasing in appearance
and manner, a brunette with large brown eyes, an imper-
tinent little nose, and a brilliant healthy colour. She was
an assistant to a milliner and bonnet-maker in the
Edgware Road.

Both these young ladies, when in the fulfilment of
their daily duties, were models of deportment; in their
hours of ease, the elder's cold dignity was rather apt to
turn to peevishness, while the younger sister, relieved
from the restraints of the showroom, betrayed a lively
and even frivolous disposition.

It was this liveliness and frivolity that had fascinated
the hairdresser in days that had gone by; but if he had
felt any self-distrust now in venturing within their influence,
such apprehensions vanished with the first sight of the
charms which had been counteracted before they had
time to prevail.

She was well enough, this Miss Ada Parkinson, he
thought now; a nice-looking girl in her way, and
stylishly dressed. But his Matilda looked twice the lady
she ever could, and a vision of his betrothed (at that
time taking a week's rest in the country) rose before
him, as if to justify and confirm his preference.

The luckless James had to undergo some amount of
scolding from Miss Bella for his want of punctuality, a
scolding which merely supplied an object to his grin;
and during her remarks, Ada had ample time to rally
Leander Tweddle upon his long neglect, and used it to
the best advantage.

Perhaps he would have been better pleased by a little less insensibility, a touch of surprise and pleasure on her part at meeting him again, as he allowed himself to show in a remark that his absence did not seem to have affected her to any great extent.

"I don't know what you expected, Mr. Tweddle," she replied. "Ought I to have cried both my eyes out? You haven't cried out either of yours, you know!"

"'Men must work, and women must weep,' as Shakspeare says," he observed, with a vague idea that he was making rather an apt quotation. But his companion pointed out that this only applied to cases where the women had something to weep about.

The party had a compartment to themselves, and Leander, who sat at one end opposite to Ada, found his spirits rising under the influence of her lively sallies.

"That's the only thing Matilda wants," he thought, "a little more liveliness and go about her. I like a little chaff myself, now and then, I must say."

At the other end of the carriage, Bella had been suggesting that the gardens might be closed so late in the year, and regretting that they had not chosen the new melodrama at the Adelphi instead; which caused Jauncy to draw glowing pictures of the attractions of Rosherwich Gardens.

"I was there a year ago last summer," he said, "and it was first-rate: open-air dancing, summer theatre, ropewalking, fireworks, and supper out under the trees. You'll enjoy yourself, Bella, right enough when you get there!"

"If that isn't enough for you, Bella," cried her sister, "you must be difficult to please! I'm sure I'm quite looking forward to it; aren't you, Mr. Tweddle?'

The poor man was cursed by the fatal desire of

pleasing, and unconsciously threw an altogether unnecessary degree of *empressement* into his voice as he replied, " In the company I am at present, I should look forward to it, if it was a wilderness with a funeral in it."

" Oh dear me, Mr. Tweddle, that *is* a pretty speech !" said Ada, and she blushed in a manner which appalled the conscience-stricken hairdresser.

" There I go again," he thought remorsefully, " putting things in the poor girl's head—it ain't right. I'm making myself too pleasant !"

And then it struck him that it would be only prudent to make his position clearly understood, and, carefully lowering his voice, he began a speech with that excellent intention. " Miss Parkinson," he said huskily, " there's something I have to tell you about myself, very particular. Since I last enjoyed the pleasure of meeting with you my prospects have greatly altered, I am no longer—— "

But she cut him short with a little gesture of entreaty. " Oh, not here, please, Mr. Tweddle," she said ; " tell me about it in the gardens !"

" Very well," he said, relieved ; " remind me when we get there—in case I forget, you know."

" Remind you !" cried Ada ; " the *idea*, Mr. Tweddle ! I certainly shan't do any such thing."

" She thinks I am going to propose to her !" he thought ruefully ; " it will be a delicate business undeceiving her. I wish it was over and done with !"

It was quite dark by the time they had crossed the river by the ferry, and made their way up to the entrance to the pleasure gardens, imposing enough, with its white colonnade, its sphinxes, and lines of coloured lamps.

But no one else had crossed with them ; and, as they stood at the turnstiles, all they could see of the grounds beyond seemed so dark and silent that they began to have involuntary misgivings. "I suppose," said Jauncy to the man at the ticket-hole, "the gardens are open—ch?"

"Oh yes," he said gruffly, "*they're* open—they're *open;* though there ain't much going on out-of-doors, being the last night of the season."

Bella again wished that they had selected the Adelphi for their evening's pleasure, and remarked that Jauncy "might have known."

"Well," said the latter to the party generally, "what do you say—shall we go in, or get back by the first train home?"

"Don't be so ridiculous, James!" said Bella, peevishly. "What's the good of going back, to be too late for everything. The mischief's done now."

"Oh, let's go in!" advised Ada; "the amusements and things will be just as nice indoors—nicer on a chilly evening like this;" and Leander seconded her heartily.

So they went in; Jauncy leading the way with the still complaining Bella, and Leander Tweddle bringing up the rear with Ada. They picked their way as well as they could in the darkness, caused by the closely planted trees and shrubs, down a winding path, where the sopped leaves gave a slippery foothold, and the branches flicked moisture insultingly in their faces as they pushed them aside.

A dead silence reigned everywhere, broken only by the wind as it rustled amongst the bare twigs, or the whistling of a flaring gas-torch protruding from some convenient tree.

Jauncy occasionally shouted back some desperate essay at jocularity, at which Ada laughed with some perseverance, until even she could no longer resist the influence of the surroundings.

On a hot summer's evening those grounds, brilliantly illuminated and crowded by holiday-makers, have been the delight of thousands of honest Londoners, and will be so again ; but it was undeniable that on this particular occasion they were pervaded by a decent melancholy.

Ada had slipped a hand, clad in crimson silk, through Leander's arm as they groped through the gloom together, and shrank to his side now and then in an alarm which was only half pretended. But if her light pressure upon his arm made his heart beat at all the faster, it was only at the fancy that the trusting hand was his Matilda's, or so at least did he account for it to himself afterwards.

They followed on, down a broad promenade, where the ground glistened with autumn damps, and the un-lighted lamps looked wan and spectral. There was a bear-pit hard by, over the railings of which Ada leaned and shouted a defiant " Boo ; " but the bears had turned in for the night, and the stone re-echoed her voice with a hollow ring. Indistinct bird forms were roosting in cages ; but her umbrella had no effect upon them.

Jauncy was waiting for them to come up, perhaps as a protection against his *fiancée's* reproaches. " In another hour," he said, with an implied apology, " you'll see how different this place looks. We—we're come a little too early. Suppose we fill up the time by a nice little dinner at the Restorong—eh, Ada ? What do you think, Tweddle ? "

The suggestion was received favourably, and Jauncy, thankful to retrieve his reputation as leader, took them towards the spot where food was to be had.

Presently they saw lights twinkling through the trees, and came to a place which was clearly the focus of festivity. There was the open-air theatre, its drop-scene lowered, its proscenium lost in the gloom ; there was the circle for *al-fresco* dancing, but it was bare, and the clustered lights were dead ; there was the restaurant, dark and silent like all else.

Jauncy stood there and rubbed his chin. " This is where I dined when we were here last," he said, at length ; "and a capital little dinner they gave us too ! "

" What *I* should like to know," said the elder Miss Parkinson, " is, where are we to dine to-night ? "

" Yes," said Jauncy, encouragingly ; " don't you fret yourself, Bella. Here's an old party sweeping up leaves, we'll ask him."

They did so, and were referred to a large building, in the Gothic style, with a Tudor doorway, known as the " Baronial All," where lights shone behind the painted windows.

Inside, a few of the lamps around the pillars were lighted, and the body of the floor was roped in as if for dancing ; but the hall was empty, save for a barmaid, assisted by a sharp little girl, behind the long bar on one of its sides.

Jauncy led his dejected little party up to this, and again put his inquiry with less hopefulness. When he found that the only available form of refreshment that evening was bitter ale and captain's biscuits, mitigated by occasional caraway seeds, he became a truly pitiable object.

" They—they don't keep this place up on the same scale in the autumn, you see," he explained weakly. " It's very different in summer ; what they call ' an endless round of amusements.' "

" There's an endless round of amusement now," observed Ada ; " but it's a naught ! "

" Oh, there'll be something going on by-and-by, never fear," said Jauncy, determined to be sanguine ; " or else they wouldn't be open."

" There'll be dancing here this evening," the barmaid informed him. " That is all we open for at this time of year ; and this is the last night of the season."

"Oh !" said Jauncy, cheerfully ; " you see we only came just in time, Bella ; and I suppose you'll have a good many down here to-night—eh, miss ? "

" How much did we take last Saturday, Jenny ? " said the barmaid to the sharp little girl.

"Seven and fourpence 'ap'ny—most of it beer," said the child. " Margaret, I may count the money again to-night, mayn't I ? "

The barmaid made some mental calculation, after which she replied to Jauncy's question. " We may have some fifteen couples or so down to-night," she said ; " but that won't be for half an hour yet."

" The question is," said Jauncy, trying to bear up under this last blow ; " the question is, How are we to amuse ourselves till the dancing begins ? "

" I don't know what others are going to do," Bella announced ; " but I shall stay here, James, and keep warm—if I can ! " and once more she uttered her regret that they had not gone to the Adelphi.

Her sister declined to follow her example. " I mean to see all there is to be seen," she declared, "since we are here ; and perhaps Mr. Tweddle will come and take care of me. Will you, Mr. Tweddle ? "

He was not sorry to comply, and they wandered out together through the grounds, which offered considerable variety. There were alleys lined with pale plaster statues, and a grove dedicated to the master minds of the world, represented by huge busts, with more or less appropriate quotations. There were alcoves, too, and neatly ruined castles.

Ada talked almost the whole time in a sprightly manner, which gave Leander no opportunity of introducing the subject of his engagement, and this continued until they had reached a small battlemented platform on some rising ground; below were the black masses of trees, with a faint fringe of light here and there; beyond lay the Thames, in which red and white reflections quivered, and from whose distant bends and reaches came the dull roar of fog-horns and the pantings of tugs.

Ada stood here in silence for some time; at last she said, " After all, I'm not sorry we came—are *you* ? "

" If I don't take care what I say, I *may* be ! " he thought, and answered guardedly, " On the contrary, I'm glad, for it gives me the opportunity of telling you something I—I think you ought to know."

" What was he going to say next ? " she thought. Was a declaration coming, and if so, should she accept him ? She was not sure; he had behaved very badly in keeping so long away from her, and a proposal would be a very suitable form of apology; but there was the gentleman who travelled for a certain firm in the Edgware Road, he had been very " particular " in his attentions of late. Well, she would see how she felt when Leander had spoken; he was beginning to speak now.

" I don't want to put it too abrupt," he said; " I'll come to it gradually. There's a young lady that I'm now looking forward to spending the whole of my future life with."

" And what is she called ? " asked Ada. (" He's rather a nice little man, after all ! " she was thinking.)

" Matilda," he said; and the answer came like a blow in the face. For the moment she hated him as bitterly as if he had been all the world to her; but she carried off her mortification by a rather hysterical laugh.

"Fancy you being engaged!" she said, by way of explanation of her merriment; "and to any one with the name of Matilda—it's such a stupid sounding sort of name!"

"It ain't at all; it all depends how you say it. If you pronounce it like I do, *Matilda*, it has rather a pretty sound. You try now."

"Well, we won't quarrel about it, Mr. Tweddle; I'm glad it isn't my name, that's all. And now tell me all about your young lady. What's her other name, and is she very good-looking?"

"She's a Miss Matilda Collum," said he; "she is considered handsome by competent judges, and she keeps the books at a florist's in the vicinity of Bayswater."

"And, if it isn't a rude question, why didn't you bring her with you this evening?"

"Because she's away for a short holiday, and isn't coming back till the last thing to-morrow night."

"And I suppose you've been wishing I was Matilda all the time?" she said audaciously; for Miss Ada Parkinson was not an over-scrupulous young person, and did not recognize in the fact of her friend's engagement any reason why she should not attempt to reclaim his vagrant admiration.

Leander *had* been guilty of this wish once or twice; but though he was not absolutely overflowing with tact, he did refrain from admitting the impeachment.

"Well, you see," he said, in not very happy evasion, "Matilda doesn't care about this kind of thing; she's rather particular, Matilda is."

"And I'm not!" said Ada. "I see; thank you, Mr. Tweddle!"

"You do take one up so!" he complained. "I never intended nothing of the sort—far from it."

"Well, then, I forgive you; we can't all be Matildas, I suppose. And now, suppose we go back; they will be beginning to dance by now!"

"With pleasure," he said; "only you must excuse me dancing, because, as an engaged man, I have had to renounce (except with one person) the charms of Terpsychore. I mean," he explained condescendingly, "that I can't dance in public save with my intended."

"Ah, well," said Ada, "perhaps Terpsy-chore will get over it; still I should like to see the Terpsy-choring, if you have no objection."

And they returned to the Baronial Hall, which by this time presented a more cheerful appearance. The lamps round the mirror-lined pillars were all lit, and the musicians were just striking up the opening bars of the Lancers; upon which several gentlemen amongst the assembly, which now numbered about forty, ran out into the open and took up positions, like colour-sergeants at drill, to be presently joined, in some bashfulness, by such ladies as desired partners.

The Lancers were performed with extreme conscientiousness; and when it was over, every gentleman with any *savoir faire* to speak of presented his partner with a glass of beer.

Then came a waltz, to which Ada beat time impatiently with her foot, and bit her lip, as she had to look on by Leander's side.

"There's Bella and James going round," she said; "I've never had to sit out a waltz before!"

He felt the implied reproach, and thought whether there could be any harm, after all, in taking a turn or two; it would be only polite. But, before he could recant in words, a soldier came up, a medium-sized warrior with a large nose and round little eyes, who had been very funny during the Lancers in directing all the figures by words of military command.

"Will you allow me the honour, miss, of just one round?" he said to Ada, respectfully enough.

The etiquette of this ballroom was not of the strictest; but she would not have consented but for the desire of showing Leander that she was not dependent upon him for her amusement. As it was, she accepted the corporal's arm a little defiantly.

Leander watched them round the hall with an odd sensation, almost of jealousy—it was quite ridiculous, because he could have danced with Ada himself had he cared to do so; and besides, it was not she, but Matilda, whom he adored.

But, as he began to notice, Ada was looking remarkably pretty that evening, and really was a partner who would bring any one credit; and her corporal danced villainously, revolving with stiff and wooden jerks, like a toy soldier. Now Leander flattered himself he could waltz—having had considerable practice in bygone days in a select assembly, where the tickets were two shillings each, and the gentlemen, as the notices said ambiguously enough, "were restricted to wearing gloves."

So he felt indignantly that Ada was not having justice done to her. "I've a good mind to give her a turn," he thought, "and show them all what waltzing is!"

Just then the pair happened to come to a halt close to him. "Shockin' time they're playing this waltz in," he heard the soldier exclaim with humorous vivacity (he was apparently the funny man of the regiment, and had brought a silent but appreciative comrade with him as audience), "abominable! excruciatin'! comic!! 'orrible!!!"

Leander seized the opportunity. "Excuse me," he said politely, "but if you don't like the music, perhaps you wouldn't mind giving up this young lady to me?"

"Oh come, I say!" said the man of war, running his fingers through his short curly hair; "my good feller, you'd better see what the lady says to that!" (He evidently had no doubt himself.)

"I'm very well content as I am, thank you all the same, Mr. Tweddle," said Ada, unkindly adding in a lower tone, "If you're so anxious to dance, dance with Terpsy-chore!"

And again he was left to watch the whirling couples with melancholy eyes. The corporal's brother-in-arms was wheeling round with a plain young person, apparently in domestic service, whose face was overspread by a large red smile of satiated ambition. James and Bella flitted by, dancing vigorously, and Bella's discontent seemed to have vanished for the time. There were jigging couples and prancing couples; couples that bounced round like imprisoned bees, and couples that glided past in calm and conscious superiority. He alone stood apart, excluded from the happy throng, and he began to have a pathetic sense of injury.

But the music stopped at last, and Ada, dismissing her partner, came towards him. "You don't seem to be enjoying yourself, Mr. Tweddle," she said maliciously.

"Don't I?" he replied. "Well, so long as you are, it don't matter, Miss Parkinson—it don't matter."

"But I'm not—at least, I didn't that dance," she said. "That soldier man did talk such rubbish, and he trod on my feet twice. I'm so hot! I wonder if it's cooler outside?"

"Will you come and see?" he suggested, and this time she did not disdain his arm, and they strolled out together.

Following a path they had hitherto left unexplored, they came to a little enclosure surrounded by tall shrubs; in the centre, upon a low pedestal, stood a female statue, upon which a gas lamp, some paces off, cast a flickering gleam athwart the foliage.

The exceptional grace and beauty of the figure would have been apparent to any lover of art. She stood there, her right arm raised, partly in gracious invitation, partly in queenly command, her left hand extended, palm downwards, as if to be reverentially saluted. The hair was parted in boldly indicated waves over the broad low brow, and confined by a fillet in a large loose knot at the back. She was clad in a long chiton, which lapped in soft zigzag folds over the girdle and fell to the feet in straight parallel lines, and a chlamys hanging from her shoulders concealed the left arm to the elbow, while it left the right arm free.

In the uncertain light one could easily fancy soft eyes swimming in those wide blank sockets, and the ripe lips were curved by a dreamy smile, at once tender and disdainful.

Leander Tweddle and Miss Ada Parkinson, however, stood before the statue in an unmoved, not to say critical, mood.

"Who's she supposed to be, I wonder?" asked the young lady, rather as if the sculptor were a harmless lunatic whose delusions took a marble shape occasionally. This, by the way, is a question which may frequently be heard in picture galleries, and implies an enlightened tolerance.

"I don't know," said Leander; "a foreign female,

I fancy—that's Russian on the pedestal." He inferred this from a resemblance to the characters on certain packets of cigarettes.

"But there's some English underneath," said Ada; "I can just make it out. Ap— Apro— Aprodyte. What a funny name!"

"You haven't prenounced it quite correckly," he said; "out there they sound the ph like a f, and give all the syllables—Afroddity." He felt a kind of intuition that this was nearer the correct rendering.

"Well," observed Ada, "she's got a silly look, don't you think?"

Leander was less narrow, and gave it as his opinion that she had been "done from a fine woman."

Ada remarked that she herself would never consent to be taken in so unbecoming a costume. "One might as well have no figure at all in things hanging down for all the world like a sack," she said.

Proceeding to details, she was struck by the smallness of the hands; and it must be admitted that, although the statue as a whole was slightly above the average female height, the arms from the elbow downwards, and particularly the hands, were by no means in proportion, and almost justified Miss Parkinson's objection, that "no woman could have hands so small as that."

"I know some one who has—quite as small," said he softly.

Ada instantly drew off one of the crimson gloves and held out her hand beside the statue's. It was a well-shaped hand, as she very well knew, but it was decidedly larger than the one with which she compared it. "I *said* so," she observed; "now are you satisfied, Mr. Tweddle?"

But he had been thinking of a hand more slender

and dainty than hers, and allowed himself to admit as much. "I—I wasn't meaning you at all," he said bluntly.

She laughed a little jarring laugh. "Oh, Matilda, of course! Nobody is like Matilda now! But come, Mr. Tweddle, you're not going to stand there and tell me that this wonderful Matilda of yours has hands no bigger than those?"

"She has been endowed with quite remarkable small hands," said he; "you wouldn't believe it without seeing. It so happens," he added suddenly, "that I can give you a very fair ideer of the size they are, for I've got a ring of hers in my pocket at this moment. It came about this way: my aunt (the same that used to let her second floor to James, and that Matilda lodges with at present), my aunt, as soon as she heard of our being engaged, nothing would do but I must give Matilda an old ring with a posy inside it, that was in our family, and we soon found the ring was too large to keep on, and I left it with old Vidler, near my place of business, to be made tighter, and called for it on my way here this very afternoon, and fortunately enough it was ready."

He took out the ring from its bed of pink cotton wool, and offered it to Miss Parkinson.

"You see if you can get it on," he said; "try the little finger!"

She drew back, offended. "*I* don't want to try it, thank you," she said (she felt as if she might fling it into the bushes if she allowed herself to touch it). "If you *must* try it on somebody, there's the statue! You'll find no difficulty in getting it on any of her fingers—or thumbs," she added.

"You shall see," said Leander. "My belief is, it's too small for her, if anything."

He was a true lover; anxious to vindicate his lady's perfections before all the world, and perhaps to convince himself that his estimate was not exaggerated. The proof was so easy, the statue's left hand hung temptingly within his reach; he accepted the challenge, and slipped the ring up the third finger, that was slightly raised as if to receive it. The hand struck no chill, so moist and mild was the evening, but felt warm and almost soft in his grasp.

"There," he said triumphantly, "it might have been made for her!"

"Well," said Ada, not too consistently, "I never said it mightn't!"

"Excuse me," said he, "but you said it would be too large for her; and, if you'll believe me, it's as much as I can do to get it off her finger, it fits that close."

"Well, make haste and get it off, Mr. Tweddle, do," said Ada, impatiently. "I've stayed out quite long enough."

"In one moment," he replied; "it's quite a job, I declare, quite a job!"

"Oh, you men are so clumsy!" cried Ada. "Let *me* try."

"No, no!" he said, rather irritably; "I can manage it," and he continued to fumble.

At last he looked over his shoulder and said, "It's a singler succumstance, but I can't get the ring past the bend of the finger."

Ada was cruel enough to burst out laughing. "It's a judgment upon you, Mr. Tweddle!" she cried.

"You dared me to it!" he retorted. "It isn't friendly of you, I must say, Miss Parkinson, to set there enjoying of it—it's bad taste!"

"Well, then, I'm very sorry, Mr. Tweddle; I won't

laugh any more; but, for goodness' sake, take me back to the Hall now."

"It's coming!" he said; "I'm working it over the joint now—it's coming quite easily."

"But I can't wait here while it comes," she said. "Do you want me to go back alone? You're not very polite to me this evening, I must say."

"What am I to do?" he said distractedly. "This ring is my engagement ring; it's valuable. I can't go away without it!"

"The statue won't run away—you can come back again, by-and-by. You don't expect me to spend the rest of the evening out here? I never thought you could be rude to a lady, Mr. Tweddle."

"No more I can," he said. "Your wishes, Miss Ada, are equivocal to commands; allow me the honour of reconducting you to the Baronial Hall."

He offered his arm in his best manner; she took it, and together they passed out of the enclosure, leaving the statue in undisturbed possession of the ring.

PLEASURE IN PURSUIT

II.

"And you, great sculptor, so you gave
A score of years to Art, her slave,
And that's your Venus, whence we turn
To yonder girl——"

ANOTHER waltz had just begun as they re-entered the Baronial Hall, and Ada glanced up at her companion from her daring brown eyes. "What would you say if I told you you might have this dance with me?" she inquired.

The hairdresser hesitated for just one moment. He had meant to leave her there and go back for his ring; but the waltz they were playing was a very enticing one. Ada was looking uncommonly pretty just then; he could get the ring equally well a few minutes later.

"I should take it very kind of you," he said, gratefully, at length.

"Ask for it, then," said Ada; and he did ask for it.

He forgot Matilda and his engagement for the moment; he sacrificed all his scruples about dancing in public; but he somehow failed to enjoy this pleasure, illicit though it was.

For one thing, he could not long keep Matilda out of his thoughts. He was doing nothing positively wrong; still, it was undeniable that she would not approve of his being there at all, still less if she knew that the gold ring given to him by his aunt for the purposes of his betrothal had been left on the finger of a foreign statue, and exposed to the mercy of any passer-by, while he waltzed with a bonnet-maker's assistant.

And his conscience was awakened still further by the discovery that Ada was a somewhat disappointing partner. "She's not so light as she used to be," he thought, "and then she jumps. I'd forgotten she jumped."

Before the waltz was nearly over he led her back to a chair, alleging as his excuse that he was afraid to abandon his ring any longer, and hastened away to the spot where it was to be found.

He went along the same path, and soon came to an enclosure; but no sooner had he entered it than he saw that he must have mistaken his way; this was not the right place. There was no statue in the middle.

He was about to turn away, when he saw something that made him start; it was a low pedestal in the centre, with the same characters upon it that he had read with Ada. It was the place, after all; yes, he could not be mistaken; he knew it now.

Where was the statue which had so lately occupied that pedestal? Had it fallen over amongst the bushes? He felt about for it in vain. It must have been removed for some purpose while he had been dancing; but by whom, and why?

The best way to find out would be to ask some one in authority. The manager was in the Baronial Hall, officiating as M.C.; he would go and inquire whether the removal had been by his orders.

He was fortunate enough to catch him as he was coming out of the hall, and he seized him by the arm with

"ANSWER ME," HE SAID ROUGHLY; "IS THIS SOME LARK
OF YOURS?" [Page 33.

nervous haste. "Mister," he began, "if you've found one of your plaster figures with a gold ring on, it's mine. I—I put it on in a joking kind of way, and I had to leave it for awhile; and now, when I come back for it, it's gone!"

"I'm sorry to hear it, sir," returned the manager; "but really, if you will leave gold rings on our statues, we can't be responsible, you know."

"But you'll excuse me," pursued Leander; "I don't think you quite understood me. It isn't only the ring that's gone—it's the statue; and if you've had it put up anywhere else——"

"Nonsense!" said the manager; "we don't move our statues about like chessmen; you've forgotten where you left it, that's all. What was the statue like?"

Leander described it as well as he could, and the manager, with a somewhat altered manner, made him point out the spot where he believed it to have stood, and they entered the grove together.

The man gave one rapid glance at the vacant pedestal, and then gripped Leander by the shoulder, and looked at him long and hard by the feeble light. "Answer me," he said, roughly; "is this some lark of yours?"

"I look larky, don't I?" said poor Tweedle, dolefully. "I thought you'd be sure to know where it was."

"I wish to heaven I did!" cried the manager, passionately; "it's those impudent blackguards. . . . They've done it under my very nose!"

"If it's any of your men," suggested Leander, "can't you make them put it back again?"

"It's not any of my men. I was warned, and, like a fool, I wouldn't believe it could be done at a time like this; and now it's too late, and what am I to say to the inspector? I wouldn't have had this happen for a thousand pounds!"

"Well, it's kind of you to feel so put out about it," said Leander. "You see, what makes the ring so valuable to me——"

The manager was pacing up and down impatiently, entirely ignoring his presence.

"I say," Tweddle repeated, "the reason why that ring's of partickler importance——"

"Oh, don't bother *me!*" said the other, shaking him off. "I don't want to be uncivil, but I've got to think this out. . . . Infernal rascals!" he went on muttering.

"Have the goodness to hear what I've got to say, though," persisted Leander. "I'm mixed up in this, whether you like it or not. You seem to know who's got this figure, and I've a right to be told too. I won't go till I get that ring back; so now you understand me!"

"Confound you and your ring!" said the manager. "What's the good of coming bully-ragging me about your ring? *I* can't get you your ring! You shouldn't have been fool enough to put it on one of our statues. You make me talk to you like this, coming bothering when I've enough on my mind as it is! Hang it! Can't you see I'm as anxious to get that statue again as ever you can be? If I don't get it, I may be a ruined man, for all I know; ain't that enough for you? Look here, take my advice, and leave me alone before we have words over this. You give me your name and address, and you may rely on hearing from me as soon as anything turns up. You can do no good to yourself or any one else by making a row; so go away quiet like a sensible chap!"

Leander felt stunned by the blow; evidently there was nothing to be done but follow the manager's advice. He went to the office with him, and gave his name and address in full, and then turned back alone to the dancing-hall.

He had lost his ring—no ordinary trinket which he could purchase anywhere, but one for which he would have to account—and to whom? To his aunt and Matilda. How could he tell, when there was even a chance of seeing it again?

If only he had not allowed himself that waltz; if only he had insisted upon remaining by the statue until his ring was removed; if only he had not been such an idiot as to put it on! None of these acts were wrong exactly; but between them they had brought him to this.

And the chief person responsible was Miss Ada Parkinson, whom he dared not reproach; for he was naturally unwilling that this last stage of the affair should become known. He would have to dissemble, and he rejoined his party with what he intended for a jaunty air.

" We've been waiting for you to go away," said Bella. " Where have you been all this time? "

He saw with relief that Ada did not appear to have mentioned the statue, and so he said he had been " strolling about."

" And Ada left to take care of herself!" said Bella, spitefully. " You are polite, Mr. Tweddle, I must say!"

" I haven't complained, Bella, that I know of," said Ada. " And Mr. Tweddle and I quite understand each other, don't we? "

" Oh!" said Bella, with an altered manner and a side-glance at James, " I didn't know. I'm very glad to hear it, I'm sure."

And then they left the gardens, and, after a substantial meal at a riverside hotel, started on the homeward journey, with the sense that their expedition had not been precisely a success.

As before, they had a railway compartment to themselves. Bella declined to talk, and lay back in her corner with closed eyes and an expression of undeserved suffering, whilst the unfortunate Jauncy sat silent and miserable opposite.

Leander would have liked to be silent too, and think out his position ; but Ada would not hear of this. Her jealous resentment had apparently vanished, and she was extremely lively and playful in her sallies.

This reached a pitch when she bent forward, and, in a whisper, which she did not, perhaps, intend to be quite confidential, said, " Oh, Mr. Tweddle, you never told me what became of the ring ! Is it off at last ? "

" Off? yes ! " he said irritably, very nearly adding, " and the statue too."

" Weren't you very glad ! " said she.

" Uncommonly," he replied grimly.

" Let me see it again, now you've got it back," she pleaded.

" You'll excuse me," he said ; " but after what has taken place, I can't show that ring to anybody."

" Then you're a cross thing ! " said Ada, pouting.

" What's the matter with you two, over there ? " asked Bella, sleepily.

Ada's eyes sparkled with mischief. " Let me tell them ; it is too awfully funny. I *must !* " she whispered to Leander. " It's all about a ring," she began, and enjoyed poor Tweddle's evident discomfort.

" A ring ? " cried Bella, waking up. " Don't keep all the fun to yourselves ; we've not had so much of it this evening."

" Miss Ada," said Leander, in great agitation, " I ask

you, as a lady, to treat what has happened this evening in the strictest confidence for the present ! "

"Secrets, Ada ? " cried her sister ; "upon my word ! "

"Why, where's the harm, Mr. Tweddle, now it's all settled ? " exclaimed Ada. "Bella, it was only this : he went and put a ring (now do wait till I've done, Mr. Tweddle !) on a certain person's finger out in those Rosherwich Gardens (you see, I've not said *whose* finger)."

"Hullo, Tweddle ! " cried Jauncy, in some bewilderment.

Leander could only cast a look of miserable appeal at him.

"Shall I tell them any more, Mr. Tweddle ? " said Ada, persistently.

" I don't think there's any necessity," he pleaded.

" No more do I," put in Bella, archly. " I think we can guess the rest."

Ada did not absolutely make any further disclosures that evening ; but for the rest of the journey she amused herself by keeping the hairdresser in perpetual torment by her pretended revelations, until he was thoroughly disgusted.

No longer could he admire her liveliness ; he could not even see that she was good-looking now. "She's nothing but chaff, chaff, chaff ! " he thought. " Thank goodness, Matilda isn't given that way. Chaff before marriage means nagging after ! "

They reached the terminus at last, when he willingly said farewell to the other three.

" Good-bye, Mr. Tweddle," said Bella, in rather a more cordial tone ; " I needn't hope *you*'ve enjoyed yourself ! "

" You needn't ! " he replied, almost savagely.

" Good night," said Ada ; and added in a whisper, " Don't go and dream of your statue-woman ! "

" If I dream to-night at all," he said, between his teeth, " it will be a nightmare ! "

" I suppose, Tweddle, old chap," said Jauncy, as he shook hands, " you know your own affairs best ; but, if you meant what you told me coming down, you've been going it, haven't you ? "

He left Leander wondering impatiently what he meant. Did he know the truth ? Well, everybody might know it before long ; there would probably be a fuss about it all, and the best thing he could do would be to tell Matilda at once, and throw himself upon her mercy. After all, it was innocent enough—if she could only be brought to believe it.

He did not look forward to telling her ; and by the time he reached the Bank and got into an omnibus, he was in a highly nervous state, as the following incident may serve to show.

He had taken one of those uncomfortable private omnibuses, where the passengers are left in unlightened gloom. He sat by the door, and, occupied as he was by his own misfortunes, paid little attention to his surroundings.

But by-and-by, he became aware that the conductor, in collecting the fares, was trying to attract the notice of some one who sat in the further corner of the vehicle. " Where are you for, lady, please ? " he asked repeatedly, and at last, " *Will* somebody ask the lady up the end where I'm to set her down ? " to all of which the eccentric person addressed returned no reply whatever.

Leander's attention was thus directed to her ; but, although in the obscurity he could make out nothing but a dim form of grey, his nerves were so unsettled that he felt a curiously uneasy fancy that eyes were being fixed upon him in the darkness.

This continued until a moment when some electric lights suddenly flashed into the omnibus as it passed, and lit up the whole interior with a ghastly glare, in which the grey female became distinctly visible.

He caught his breath and shrank into the corner; for in that moment his excited imagination had traced a strange resemblance to the figure he had left in Rosherwich Gardens. The inherent improbability of finding a classical statue seated in an omnibus did not occur to him, in the state his mind was in just then. He sat there fascinated, until lights shone in once more, and he saw, or thought he saw, the figure slowly raise her hand and beckon to him.

That was enough; he started up with a smothered cry, thrust a coin into the conductor's hand, and, without waiting for change, flung himself from the omnibus in full motion.

When its varnished sides had ceased to gleam in the light of the lamps, and its lumbering form had been swallowed up in the autumn haze, he began to feel what a coward his imagination had made of him.

" My nightmare's begun already," he thought. " Still, she was so surprisingly like, it did give me a turn. They oughtn't to let such crazy females into public conveyances ! "

Fortunately his panic had not seized him until he was within a short distance from Bloomsbury, and it did not take him long to reach Queen Square and his shop in the passage. He let himself in, and went up to a little room on an upper floor, which he used as his sitting-room. The person who " looked after him " did not sleep on the premises; but she had laid a fire and left out his tea-things. "I'll have some tea," he thought, as he lit the gas and saw them there. "I feel as if I want cheering up, and it can't make me any more shaky than I am."

And when his fire was crackling and blazing up, and his kettle beginning to sing, he felt more cheerful already. What, after all, if it did take some time to get his ring again? He must make some excuse or other; and, should the worst come to the worst, "I suppose," he thought, "I could get another made like it—though, when I come to think of it, I'll be shot if I remember exactly what it was like, or what the words inside it were, to be sure about them; still, very likely old Vidler would recollect, and I dessay it won't turn out to be necessa—— What the devil's that?"

He had the house to himself after nightfall, and he remembered that his private door could not be opened now without a special key; yet he could not help a fancy that some one was groping his way up the staircase outside.

"It's only the boards creaking, or the pipes leaking through," he thought. "I must have the place done up. But I'm as nervous as a cat to-night."

The steps were nearer and nearer—they stopped at the door—there was a loud commanding blow on the panels.

"Who's here at this time of night?" cried Leander, aloud. "Come in, if you want to!"

But the door remained shut, and there came another rap, even more imperious.

"I shall go mad if this goes on!" he muttered, and making a desperate rush to the door, threw it wide open, and then staggered back panic-stricken.

Upon the threshold stood a tall figure in classical

drapery. His eyes might have deceived him in the omnibus ; but here, in the crude gaslight, he could not be mistaken. It was the statue he had last seen in Rosherwich Gardens—now, in some strange and wondrous way, moving—alive !

A DISTINGUISHED STRANGER

III.

"How could it be a dream? Yet there
She stood, the moveless image fair!"

The Earthly Paradise.

WITH slow and stately tread the statue advanced towards the centre of the hairdresser's humble sitting-room, and stood there awhile, gazing about her with something of scornful wonder in her calm cold face. As she turned her head, the wide, deeply-cut sockets seemed the home of shadowy eyes; her face, her bared arms, and the long straight folds of her robe were all of the same greyish-yellow hue; the boards creaked under her sandalled feet, and Leander felt that he had never heard of a more appallingly massive ghost—if ghost indeed she were.

He had retired step by step before her to the hearth-rug, where he now stood shivering, with the fire hot at his back, and his kettle still singing on undismayed. He made no attempt to account for her presence there on any rationalistic theory. A statue had suddenly come to life, and chosen to pay him a nocturnal visit; he knew no more than that, except that he would have given worlds for courage to show it the door.

The spectral eyes were bent upon him, as if in

expectation that he would begin the conversation, and, at last, with a very unmanageable tongue, he managed to observe—

"Did you want to see me on—on business, mum?"

But the statue only relaxed her lips in a haughty smile.

"For goodness' sake, say something!" he cried wildly; "unless you want me to jump out of the winder! What is it you've come about?"

It seemed to him that in some way a veil had lifted from the stone face, leaving it illumined by a strange light, and from the lips came a voice which addressed him in solemn far-away tones, as of one talking in sleep. He could not have said with certainty that the language was his own, though somehow he understood her perfectly.

"You know me not?" she said, with a kind of sad indifference.

"Well," Leander admitted, as politely as his terror would allow, "you certingly have the advantage of me for the moment, mum."

"I am Aphrodite the foam-born, the matchless seed of Ægis-bearing Zeus. Many names have I amongst the sons of men, and many temples, and I sway the hearts of all lovers; and gods—yea, and mortals—have burned for me, a goddess, with an unconsuming, unquenchable fire!"

"Lor!" said Leander. If he had not been so much flurried, he might have found a remark worthier of the occasion, but the announcement that she was a goddess took his breath away. He had quite believed that goddesses were long since "gone out."

"You know wherefore I am come hither?" she said.

"DID YOU WANT TO SEE ME ON—ON BUSINESS, MUM?"

[*Page* 46.

"Not at this minute, I don't," he replied. "You'll excuse me, but you can't be the statue out of those gardens? You reelly are so surprisingly like, that I couldn't help asking you."

"I am Aphrodite, and no statue. Long—how long I know not—have I lain entranced in slumber in my sea-girt isle of Cyprus, and now again has the living touch of a mortal hand upon one of my sacred images called me from my rest, and given me power to animate this marble shell. Some hand has placed this ring upon my finger. Tell me, was it yours?"

Leander was almost reassured; after all, he could forgive her for terrifying him so much, since she had come on so good-natured an errand.

"Quite correct, mum—miss!" (he wished he knew the proper form for addressing a goddess) "that ring is my property. I'm sure it's very civil and friendly of you to come all this way about it," and he held out his hand for it eagerly.

"And think you it was for this that I have visited the face of the earth and the haunts of men, and followed your footsteps hither by roads strange and unknown to me? You are too modest, youth."

"I don't know what there is modest in expecting you to behave honest!" he said, rather wondering at his own audacity.

"How are you called?" she inquired suddenly on this; and after hearing the answer, remarked that the name was known to her as that of a goodly and noble youth who had perished for the sake of Hero.

"The gentleman may have been a connection of mine, for all I know," he said; "the Tweddles have always kep' themselves respectable. But I'm not a hero myself, I'm a hairdresser."

49

She repeated the word thoughtfully, though she did not seem to quite comprehend it; and indeed it is likely enough that, however intelligible she was to Leander, the understanding was far from being entirely reciprocal.

She extended her hand to him, smiling not ungraciously. "Leander," she said, "cease to tremble, for a great happiness is yours. Bold have you been; yet am I not angered, for I come. Cast, then, away all fear, and know that Aphrodite disdains not to accept a mortal's plighted troth!"

Leander entrenched himself promptly behind the armchair. "I don't know what you're talking about!" he said. "How can I help fearing, with you coming down on me like this? Ask yourself."

"Can you not understand that your prayer is heard?" she demanded.

"*What* prayer?" cried Leander.

"Crass and gross-witted has the world grown!" said she; "a Greek swain would have needed but few words to divine his bliss. Know, then, that your suit is accepted; never yet has Aphrodite turned the humblest from her shrine. By this symbol," and she lightly touched the ring, "you have given yourself to me. I accept the offering—you are mine!"

Leander was stupefied by such an unlooked-for misconception. He could scarcely believe his ears; but he hastened to set himself right at once.

"If you mean that you were under the impression that I meant anything in particular by putting that ring on, it was all a mistake, mum," he said. "I shouldn't have presumed to it!"

"Were you the lowliest of men, I care not," she replied; "to you I owe the power I now enjoy of life and vision, nor shall you find me ungrateful. But forbear

50

this false humility ; I like it not. Come, then, Leander, at the bidding of Cypris ; come, and fear nothing ! "

But he feared very much, for he had seen the operas of *Don Giovanni* and *Zampa*, and knew that any familiarity with statuary was likely to have unpleasant consequences. He merely strengthened his defences with a chair.

" You must excuse me, mum, you must indeed," he faltered ; " I can't come ! "

" Why ? " she asked.

" Because I've other engagements," he replied.

" I remember," she said slowly, " in the grove, when light met my eyes once more, there was a maid with you, one who laughed and was merry. Answer—is she your love ? "

" No, she isn't," he said shortly. " What if she was ? "

" If she were," observed the goddess, with the air of one who mentioned an ordinary fact, " I should crush her ! "

" Lord bless me ! " cried Leander, in his horror. " What for ? "

" Would not she be in my path ? and shall any mortal maid stand between me and my desire ? "

This was a discovery. She was a jealous and vengeful goddess ; she would require to be sedulously humoured, or harm would come.

" Well, well," he said soothingly, " there's nothing of that sort about her, I do assure you."

" Then I spare her," said the goddess. " But how, then, if this be truly so, do you still shrink from the honour before you ? "

Leander felt a natural unwillingness to explain that it was because he was engaged to a young lady who kept the accounts at a florist's.

"Well, the fact is," he said awkwardly, "there's difficulties in the way."

"Difficulties? I can remove them all!" she said.

"Not *these* you can't, mum. It's like this: You and me, we don't start, so to speak, from the same basin. I don't mean it as any reproach to you, but you can't deny you're an Eathen, and, worse than that, an Eathen goddess. Now all my family have been brought up as chapel folk, Primitive Methodists, and I've been trained to have a horror of superstition and idolatries, and see the folly of it. So you can see for yourself that we shouldn't be likely to get on together!"

"You talk words," she said impatiently; "but empty are they, and meaningless to my ears. One thing I learn from them—that you seek to escape me!"

"That's putting it too harsh, mum," he protested. "I'm sure I feel the honour of such a call; and, by the way, do you mind telling me how you got my address— how you found me out, I mean?"

"No one remains long hid from the searching eye of the high gods," she replied.

"So I should be inclined to say," agreed Leander. "But only tell me this, wasn't it you in the omnibus? We call our public conveyances omnibuses, as perhaps you mayn't know."

"I, sea-born Aphrodite, *I* in a public conveyance, an omnibus? There is an impiety in such a question!"

"Well, I only thought it might have been," he stammered, rather relieved upon the whole that it was not the goddess who had seen his precipitate bolt from the vehicle. Who the female in the corner really was, he never knew; though a man of science might account for the resemblance she bore to the statue by ascribing it to one of those preparatory impressions projected occasionally by a strong personality upon a weak one. But Leander was content to leave the matter unexplained.

"Let it suffice you," she said, "that I am here ; and once more, Leander, are you prepared to fulfil the troth you have plighted ? "

"I—I can't say I am," he said. "Not that I don't feel thankful for having had the refusal of so very 'igh-class an opportunity ; but, as I'm situated at present— what with the state of trade, and unbelief so rampant, and all—I'm obliged to decline with respectful thanks."

He trusted that after this she would see the propriety of going.

"Have a care ! " she said ; "you are young and not uncomely, and my heart pities you. Do nothing rash. Pause, ere you rouse the implacable ire of Aphrodite ! "

"Thank you," said Leander ; "if you'll allow me, I will. I don't want any ill-feeling, I'm sure. It's my wish to live peaceable with all men."

"I leave you, then. Use the time before you till I come again in thinking well whether he acts wisely who spurns the proffered hand of Idalian Aphrodite. For the present, farewell, Leander ! "

He was overjoyed at his coming deliverance. "Good evening, mum," he said, as he ran to the door and held it open. "If you'll allow me, I'll light you down the staircase—it's rather dark, I'm afraid."

"*Fool!*" she said with scorn, and without stirring from her place ; and, as she spoke the word, the veil seemed to descend over her face again, the light faded out, and, with a slight shudder, the figure imperceptibly resumed its normal attitude, the drapery stiffened once more into chiselled folds, and the statue was soulless as are statues generally.

FROM BAD TO WORSE

E.

IV.

"And the shadow flits and fleets,
And will not let me be,
And I loathe the squares and streets!"

Maud.

For some time after the statue had ceased to give signs of life, the hairdresser remained gaping, incapable of thought or action. At last he ventured to approach cautiously, and on touching the figure, found it perfectly cold and hard. The animating principle had plainly departed, and left the statue a stone.

"She's gone," he said, "and left her statue behind her! Well, of all the *goes*—— She's come out without her pedestal, too! To be sure, it would have been in her way, walking."

Seating himself in his shabby old armchair, he tried to collect his scattered wits. He scarcely realised, even yet, what had happened; but, unless he had dreamed it all, he had been honoured by the marked attentions of a marble statue, instigated by a heathen goddess, who insisted that his affections were pledged to her.

Perhaps there was a spice of flattery in such a situation—for it cannot fall to the lot of many hairdressers to be thus distinguished—but Leander was far too much alarmed to appreciate it. There had been suggestions of menace in the statue's remarks which made him shudder when he recalled them, and he started violently once or twice when some wavering of the light gave a play of life to the marble mask. "She's coming back!" he thought. "Oh, I do wish she wouldn't!" But Aphrodite continued immovable, and at last he concluded that, as he put it, she "had done for the evening."

His first reflection was—what had best be done? The wisest course seemed to be to send for the manager of the gardens, and restore the statue while its animation was suspended. The people at the gardens would take care that it did not get loose again.

But there was the ring; he must get that off first. Here was an unhoped-for opportunity of accomplishing this in privacy, and at his leisure. Again approaching the figure, he tried to draw off the compromising circle ; but it seemed tighter than ever, and he drew out a pair of scissors and, after a little hesitation, respectfully inserted it under the hoop and set to work to prize it off, with the result of snapping both the points, and leaving the ring entirely unaffected. He glanced at the face ; it wore the same dreamy smile, with a touch of gentle contempt in it. "She don't seem to mind," he said aloud ; "to be sure, she ain't inside of it now, as far as I make it out. I've got all night before me to get the confounded thing off, and I'll go on till I've done it !"

But he laboured on with the disabled scissors, and only succeeded in scratching the smooth marble a little ; he stopped to pant. "There's only way," he told himself desperately ; "a little diamond cement would make it all right again ; and you expect cracks in a statue."

Then, after a furtive glance around, he fetched the poker from the fireplace. He felt horribly brutal, as if he were going to mutilate and maltreat a creature that could feel; but he nerved himself to tap the back of Aphrodite's hand at the dimpled base of the third finger. The shock ran up to his elbow, and gave him acute " pins and needles," but the stone hand was still intact. He struck again—this time with all his force—and the poker flew from his grasp, and his arm dropped paralyzed by his side.

He could scarcely lift it again for some minutes, and the warning made him refrain from any further violence. " It's no good," he groaned. " If I go on, I don't know what may happen to me. I must wait till she comes to, and then ask her for the ring, very polite and civil, and try if I can't get round her that way."

He was determined that he would never give her up to the gardens while she wore his ring; but, in the mean time, he could scarcely leave the statue standing in the middle of his sitting-room, where it would most assuredly attract the charwoman's attention.

He had little cupboards on each side of his fireplace: one of these had no shelves, and served for storing fire-wood and bottles of various kinds. From this he removed the contents, and lifting the statue, which, possibly because its substance had been affected in some subtle and inexplicable manner by the vital principle that had so lately permeated it, proved less ponderous than might have been reasonably expected, he pushed it well into the recess, and turned the key on it.

Then he went trembling to bed, and, after an interval of muddled, anxious thinking, fell into a heavy sleep, which lasted until far into the morning.

He woke with the recollection that something unpleasant was hanging over him, and by degrees he remembered what that something was; but it looked so extravagant in the morning light that he had great hopes all would turn out to be a mere dream.

It was a mild Sunday morning, and there were church bells ringing all around him; it seemed impossible that he could really be harbouring an animated antique. But to remove all doubt, he stole down, half dressed, to his small sitting-room, which he found looking as usual—the fire burning dull and dusty in the sunlight that struck in through the open window, and his breakfast laid out on the table.

Almost reassured, he went to the cupboard and unlocked the door. Alas! it held its skeleton—the statue was there, preserving the attitude of queenly command in which he had seen it first. Sharply he shut the door again, and turned the key with a heavy heart.

He swallowed his breakfast with very little appetite, after which he felt he could not remain in the house. "To sit here with *that* in the cupboard is more than I'm equal to all Sunday," he decided.

If Matilda had been at his aunt's, with whom she lodged, he would have gone to chapel with her; but Matilda did not return from her holiday till late that night. He thought of going to his friend and asking his advice on his case. James, as a barrister's clerk, would presumably be able to give a sound legal opinion on an emergency.

James, however, lived "out Camden Town way," and was certain on so fine a morning to be away on some Sunday expedition with his betrothed: it was hopeless to go in search of him now. If he went to see his aunt, who lived close by in Millman Street, she might ask him about the ring, and there would be a fuss. He was in no humour for attending any place of public worship, and so he spent some hours in aimless wandering about the streets, which, as foreigners are fond of reminding us, are not exhilarating even on the brightest Sabbath, and did not raise his spirits then.

At last hunger drove him back to the passage in Southampton Row, the more quickly as it began to occur to him that the statue might possibly have revived, and be creating a disturbance in the cupboard.

He had passed the narrow posts, and was just taking out his latchkey, when some one behind touched his shoulder and made him give a guilty jump. He dreaded to find the goddess at his elbow; however, to his relief, he found a male stranger, plainly and respectably dressed.

" You Mr. Tweddle the hairdresser ? " the stranger inquired.

Leander felt a wild impulse to deny it, and declare that he was his own friend, and had come to see himself on business, for he was in no social mood just then ; but he ended by admitting that he supposed he was Mr. Tweddle.

" So did I. Well, I want a little private talk with you, Mr. Tweddle. I've been hanging about for some time ; but though I knocked and rang, I couldn't make a soul hear."

" There isn't a soul inside," protested Tweddle, with unnecessary warmth ; " not a solitary soul ! You wanted to talk with me. Suppose we take a turn round the square ? "

" No, no. I won't keep you out ; I'll come in with you ! "

Inwardly wondering what his visitor wanted, Leander led him in and lit the gas in his hair-cutting saloon. " We shall be cosier here," he said ; for he dared not take the stranger up in the room where the statue was concealed, for fear of accidents.

The man sat down in the operating-chair and crossed his legs. "I dare say you're wondering what I've come about like this on a Sunday afternoon?" he began.

"Not at all," said Leander. "Anything I can have the pleasure of doing for you——"

"It's only to answer a few questions. I understand you lost a ring at the Rosherwich Gardens yesterday evening: that's so, isn't it?"

He was a military looking person, as Leander now perceived, and he had a close-trimmed iron-grey beard, a high colour, quick eyes, and a stiff hard-lipped mouth—not at all the kind of man to trifle with. And yet Leander felt no inclination to tell him his story; the stranger might be a reporter, and his adventure would "get into the papers"—perhaps reach Matilda's eyes.

"I—I dropped a ring last night, certainly," he said; "it may have been in the gardens, for what I know."

"Now, now," said the stranger, "don't you *know* it was in the gardens? Tell me all about it."

"Begging your pardon," said Leander, "I should like to know first what call you have to *be* told."

"You're quite right—perfectly right. I always deal straightforwardly when I can. I'll tell you who I am. I'm Inspector Bilbow, of the Criminal Investigation Department, Scotland Yard. Now, perhaps, you'll see I'm not a man to be kept in the dark. And I want you to tell me when and where you last saw that ring of yours: it's to your own interest, if you want to see it again."

But Leander *had* seen it again, and it seemed certain that all Scotland Yard could not assist him in getting it back; he must manage it single-handed.

"It's very kind of you, Mr. Inspector, to try and find it for me," he said; "but the fact is, it—it ain't so valuable as I fancied. I can't afford to have it traced—it's not worth it!"

The inspector laughed. "I never said it was, that I know. The job I'm in charge of is a bigger concern than your trumpery ring, my friend."

"Then I don't see what I've got to do with it," said Leander.

The officer had taken his measure by this time; he must admit his man into a show of confidence, and appeal to his vanity, if he was to obtain any information he could rely upon.

"You're a shrewd chap, I see; 'nothing for nothing' is your motto, eh? Well, if you help me in this, and put me on the track I want, it'll be a fine thing for you. You'll be a principal witness at the police-court; name in the papers; regular advertisement for you!"

This prospect, had he known it—but even inspectors cannot know everything—was the last which could appeal to Leander in his peculiar position. "I don't care for notoriety," he said loftily; "I scorn it."

"Oho!" said the inspector, shifting his ground. "Well, you don't want to impede the course of justice, do you?—because that's what you seem to me to be after, and you won't find it pay in the long run. I'll get this out of you in a friendly way if I can; if not, some other way. Come, give me your account, fair and full, of how you came to lose that ring; there's no help for it—you must!"

Leander saw this and yielded. After all, it did not much matter, for of course he would not touch upon the strange sequel of his ill-omened act; so he told the story faithfully and circumstantially, while the inspector took it all down in his note-book, questioning him closely respecting the exact time of each occurrence.

At last he closed his note-book with a snap. "I'm not obliged to tell you anything in return for all this," he said; "but I will, and then you'll see the importance of holding your tongue till I give you leave to talk about it."

"*I* shan't talk about it," said Leander.

"I don't advise you to. I suppose you've heard of that affair at Wricklesmarsh Court? What! not that business where a gang broke into the sculpture gallery, one of the finest private collections in England? You surprise me!"

"And what did they steal?" asked Leander.

"They stole the figure whose finger you were ass enough (if you'll allow me the little familiarity) to put your ring on. What do you think of that?"

A wild rush of ideas coursed through the hairdresser's head. Was this policeman "after" the goddess upstairs? Did he know anything more? Would it be better to give up the statue at once and get rid of it? But then—his ring would be lost for ever!

"It's surprising," he said at last. "But what did they want to go and burgle a plaster figure for?"

"That's where it is, you see; she ain't plaster—she's marble, a genuine antic of Venus, and worth thousands. The beggars who broke in knew that, and took nothing else. They'd made all arrangements to get away with her abroad, and pass her off on some foreign collection before it got blown upon; and they'd have done it too if we hadn't been beforehand with them! So what do they do then? They drive up with her to these gardens, ask to see the manager, and say they're agents for some Fine Arts business, and have a sample with them, to be disposed of at a low price. The manager, so he tells me, had a look at it, thought it a neat article and suitable to the style of his gardens. He took it to be plain plaster, as they said, and they put it up for him their own selves, near the small gate up by the road; then they took the money—a pound or two they asked for it—and drove away, and he saw no more of them."

"And was that all they got for their pains?" said Leander.

The inspector smiled indulgently. "Don't you see your way yet?" he asked. "Can't you give a guess where that statue's got to now, eh?"

"No," said Leander, with what seemed to the inspector a quite uncalled-for excitement, "of course I can't! What do you ask me for? How should I know?"

"Quite so," said the other; "you want a mind trained to deal with these things. It may surprise you to hear it, but I know as well how that statue disappeared, and what was done with her, as if I'd been there!"

"Do you, though?" thought Leander, who was beginning to doubt whether his visitor's penetration was anything so abnormal. "What was done with her?" he asked.

"Why, it was a plant from the first. They knew all their regular holes were stopped, and they wanted a place to dump her down in, where she wouldn't attract attention, till they could call for her again; so they got her taken in at the gardens, where they could come in any time by the gate and fetch her off again—and very neatly it was done, too!"

"But where do you make out they've taken her to now?" asked Leander, who was naturally anxious to discover if the official had any suspicions of him.

"I've my own theory about that," was his answer. "I shall hunt that Venus down, sir; I'll stake my reputation on it."

"Venus is her name, it seems," thought Leander. "She told me it was Aphrodite. But perhaps the other's her Christian name. It can't be the Venus I've seen pictures of—she's dressed too decent."

"Yes," repeated the inspector, " I shall hunt her down now. I don't envy the poor devil who's giving her house-room ; he'll have reason to repent it !"

"How do you know any one's giving her house-room ? " inquired Leander; " and why should he repent it ? "

"Ask your own common sense. They daren't take her back to any of their own places; they know better. They haven't left the country with her. What remains ? They've bribed or got over some mug of an outsider to be their accomplice, and a bad speculation he'll find it, too."

"What would be done to him ? " asked the hair-dresser, with a quite unpleasant internal sensation.

"That is a question I wouldn't pretend to decide ; but I've no hesitation in saying that the party on whose premises that statue is discovered will wish he'd died before he ever set eyes on her."

"You're quite right there ! " said Leander. " Well, sir, I'm afraid I haven't been much assistance to you."

"Never mind that," said the inspector, encouragingly ; " you've answered my questions ; you've not hindered the law, and that's a game some burn their fingers at."

Leander let him out, and returned to his saloon with his head in a worse whirl than before. He did not think the detective suspected him. He was clearly barking up the wrong tree at present; but so acute a mind could not be long deceived, and if once Leander was implicated his guilt would appear beyond denial. Would the police believe that the statue had run after him? No one

"WHAT WOULD BE DONE TO HIM?" ASKED THE HAIRDRESSER, WITH
A QUITE UNPLEASANT INTERNAL SENSATION.   [*Page* 66.

would believe it! To be found in possession of that fatal work of art would inevitably ruin him.

He might carry her away to some lonely spot and leave her, but where was the use? She would only come back again; or he might be taken in the act. He dared not destroy her; his right arm had been painful all day after that last attempt.

If he gave her up to the authorities, he would have to explain how he came to be in a position to do so, which, as he now saw, would be a difficult undertaking; and even then he would lose all chance of recovering his ring in time to satisfy his aunt and Matilda. There was no way out of it, unless he could induce Venus to give up the token and leave him alone.

"Cuss her!" he said angrily; "a pretty bog she's led me into, she and that minx, Ada Parkinson!"

He felt so thoroughly miserable that hunger had vanished, and he dreaded the idea of an evening at home, though it was a blusterous night, with occasional vicious spirts of rain, and by no means favourable to continued pacing of streets and squares.

"I'm hanged if I don't think I'll go to church!" he thought; "and perhaps I shall feel more equal to supper afterwards."

He went upstairs to get his best hat and overcoat, and was engaged in brushing the former in his sitting-room, when from within the cupboard he heard a shower of loud raps.

His knees trembled. "She's wuss than any ghost!" he thought; but he took no notice, and went on brushing his hat, while he endeavoured to hum a hymn.

"Leander!" cried the clear, hard voice he knew too well, "I have returned. Release me!"

His first idea was to run out of the house and seek

sanctuary in some pew in the opposite church. " But there," he thought disgustedly, " she'd only come in and sit next to me. No, I'll pluck up a spirit and have it out with her ! " and he threw open the door.

" How have you dared to imprison me in this narrow tomb ? " she demanded majestically, as she stepped forth.

Leander cringed. " It's a nice roomy cupboard," he said. " I thought perhaps you wouldn't mind putting up with it, especially as you invited yourself," he could not help adding.

" When I found myself awake and in utter darkness," she said, " I thought you had buried me beneath the soil."

" Buried you ! " he exclaimed, with a sudden perception that he might do worse.

" And in that thought I was preparing to invoke the forces that lie below the soil to come to my aid, burst the masses that impeded me, and overwhelm you and all this ugly swarming city in one vast ruin ! "

" I won't bury her," Leander decided. " I'm sorry you hadn't a better opinion of me, mum," he said aloud. " You see, how you came to be in there was this way : when you went out, like the snuff of a candle, so to speak, you left your statue standing in the middle of the floor, and I had to put it somewhere where it wouldn't be seen."

" You did well," she said indulgently, " to screen my image from the vulgar sight ; and if you had no statelier shrine wherein to instal it, the fault lies not with you. You are pardoned."

" Thank you, mum," said Leander ; " and now let me ask you if you intend to animate that statue like this as a regular thing ? "

70

"So long as your obstinacy continues, or until it out-lives my forbearance, I shall return at intervals," she said. "Why do you ask this?"

"Well," said Leander, with a sinking heart, but hoping desperately to move her by the terrors of the law, "it's my duty to tell you that that image you're in is stolen property."

"Has it been stolen from one of my temples?" she asked.

"I dare say—I don't know; but there's the police moving heaven and earth to get you back again!"

"He is good and pious—the police, and if I knew him I would reward him."

"There's a good many hims in the police—that's what we call our guards for the street, who take up thieves and bad characters; and, being stolen, they're all of 'em after *you;* and if they had a notion where you were, they'd be down on you, and back you'd go to wherever you've come from—some gallery, I believe, where you wouldn't get away again in a hurry! Now, I tell you what it is, if you don't give me up that ring, and go away and leave me in quiet, I'll tell the police who you are and where you are. I mean what I say, by George I do!"

"We know not George, nor will it profit you to invoke him now," said the goddess. "See, I will deign to reason with you as with some froward child. Think you that, should the guards seize my image, *I* should remain within, or that it is aught to me where this marble presentment finds a resting-place while I am absent therefrom? But for you, should you surrender it into their hands, would there be no punishment for your im-piety in thus concealing a divine effigy?"

"She ain't no fool!" thought Leander; "she mayn't

understand our ways, but she's a match for me notwithstanding. I must try another line."

"Lady Venus," he began, "if that's the proper way to call you, I didn't mean any threats—far from it. I'll be as humble as you please. You look a good-natured lady; you wouldn't want to make a man uncomfortable, I'm sure. Do give me back that ring, for mercy's sake! If I haven't got it to show in a day or two, I shall be ruined!"

"Should any mortal require the ring of you, you have but to reply, 'I have placed it upon the finger of Aphrodite, whose spouse I am!' Thus will you have honour amongst mortals, being held blameless!"

"Blameless!" cried Leander, in pardonable exasperation. "That's all you know about it! And what am I to say to the lady it lawfully belongs to?"

"You have lied to me, then, and you are already affianced! Tell me the abode of this maiden of yours."

"What do you want it for?" he inquired, hoping faintly she might intend to restore the ring.

"To seek it out, to go to her abode, to crush her! Is she not my rival?"

"Crush my Matilda?" he cried in agony. "You'll never do such a thing as that?"

"You have revealed her name! I have but to ask in your streets, 'Where abideth Matilda, the beloved of Leander, the dresser of hair? Lead me to her dwelling.' And having arrived thereat, I shall crush her, and thus she shall deservedly perish!"

He was horrified at the possible effects of his slip, which he hastened to repair. "You won't find it so easy to come at her, luckily," he said; "there's hundreds of Matildas in London alone."

"Then," said the goddess, sweetly and calmly, "it is simple: I shall crush them all."

"Oh, lor!" whimpered Leander, "here's a blood-thirsty person! Where's the sense of doing that?"

"Because, dissipated reveller that you are, you love them."

"Now, when did I ever say I loved them? I don't even know more than two or three, and those I look on as sisters—in fact" (here he hit upon a lucky evasion) "they *are* sisters—it's only another name for them. I've a brother and three Matildas, and here are you talking of crushing my poor sisters as if they were so many beadles —all for nothing!"

"Is this the truth? Palter not with me! You are pledged to no mortal bride?"

"I'm a bachelor. And as for the ring, it belongs to my aunt, who's over fifty."

"Then no one stands between us, and you are mine!"

"Don't talk so ridiculous! I tell you I ain't yours— it's a free country, this is!"

"If I—an immortal—can stoop thus, it becomes you not to reject the dazzling favour."

A last argument occurred to him. "But I reelly don't think, mum," he said persuasively, "that you can be quite aware of the extent of the stoop. The fact is, I am, as I've tried to make you understand, a hairdresser; some might lower themselves so far as to call me a barber. Now, hairdressing, whatever may be said for it" (he could not readily bring himself to decry his profession)—"hair-dressing is considribly below you in social rank. I wouldn't deceive you by saying otherwise. I assure you that, if you had any ideer what a barber was, you wouldn't be so pressing."

F

She seemed to be struck by this. " You say well ! " she observed, thoughtfully; " your occupation may be base and degrading, and if so, it were well for me to know it."

"If you were once to see me in my daily avocations," he urged, " you'd see what a mistake you're making."

" Enough ! I will see you—and at once. Barb, that I may know the nature of your toil ! "

" I can't do that now," he objected ; " I haven't got a customer."

" Then fetch one, and barb with it immediately. You must have your tools by you; so delay not ! "

" A customer ain't a tool ! " he groaned, " it's a fellow-man ; and no one will come in to-night, because it's Sunday. (Don't ask me what Sunday is, because you wouldn't understand if I tried to tell you !) And I don't carry on my business up here, but below in the saloon."

" I will go thither and behold you."

" No ! " he exclaimed. " Do you want to ruin me ? "

" I will make no sign ; none shall recognise me for what I am. But come I will ! "

Leander pondered awhile. There was danger in introducing the goddess into his saloon ; he had no idea what she might do there. But at the same time, if she were bent upon coming, she would probably do so in any case ; and besides, he felt tolerably certain that what she would see would convince her of his utter unsuitability as a consort.

Yes, it was surely wisest to assist necessity, and obtain the most favourable conditions for the inevitable experiment.

" I might put you in a corner of the operating-room, to be sure," he said thoughtfully. " No one would think but what you was part of the fittings, unless you went moving about.'

" Place me where I may behold you at your labour, and there I will remain," she said.

" Well," he conceded, " I'll risk it. The best way would be for you to walk down to the saloon, and leave yourself ready in a corner till you come to again. I can't carry a heavy marble image all that way ! "

" So be it," said she, and followed him to the saloon with a proud docility.

" It's nicely got up," he remarked, as they reached it ; " and you'll find it roomier than the cupboard."

She deigned no answer as she remained motionless in the corner he had indicated ; and presently, as he held up the candle he was carrying, he found its rays were shining upon a senseless stone.

He went upstairs again, half fearful, half sanguine. " I don't altogether like it," he was thinking. " But if I put a print wrapper over her all day, no one will notice. And goddesses must have their proper pride. If she once gets it into her marble head that I keep a shop, I think that she'll turn up her nose at me. And then she'll give back the ring and go away, and I shan't be afraid of the police ; and I needn't tell Tillie anything about it. It's worth risking."

AN EXPERIMENT

V.

"'Tis time ; descend ; be stone no more ; approach :
   Strike all that look upon with marvel."

The Winter's Tale.

THE next day brought Leander a letter which made his heart beat with mingled emotions—it was from his Matilda. It had evidently been written immediately before her return, and told him that she would be at their old meeting-place (the statue of Fox in Bloomsbury Square) at eight o'clock that evening.

The wave of tenderness which swept over him at the anticipation of this was hurled back by an uncomfortable thought. What if Matilda were to refer to the ring ? But no ; his Matilda would do nothing so indelicate.

All through the day he mechanically went through his hairdressing, singeing, and shampooing operations, divided between joy at the prospect of seeing his adored Matilda again, and anxiety respecting the cold marble swathed in the print wrapper, which stood in the corner of his hair-cutting saloon.

He glanced at it every time he went past to change a brush or heat a razor, but there was no sign of movement under the folds, and he gradually became reassured, especially as it excited no remark.

But as evening drew on he felt that, for the success of

his experiment, it was necessary that the cover should be removed. It was dangerous, supposing the inspector were to come in unexpectedly and recognise the statue; but he could only trust to fortune for that, and hoped, too, that even if the detective came he would be able to keep him in the outer shop.

It was only for one evening, and it was well worth the risk.

A foreign gentleman had come in, and the hairdresser found that a fresh wrapper was required, which gave him the excuse he wanted for unveiling the Aphrodite. He looked carefully at the face as he uncovered it, but could discover no speculation as yet in the calm, full gaze of the goddess.

The foreign gentleman was inclined to be talkative under treatment, and the conversation came round to public amusements.

" In my country," the customer said, without mentioning or betraying what his particular country was—" in my country we have what you have not, places to sit out in the fresh air, and drink a glass of beer, along with the entertainments. You have not that in London?"

" Bless your soul, yes," said Leander, who was a true patriot, " plenty of them!"

" Oh, I did not aware that; but who?"

" Well," said the hairdresser, " there's the Eagle in the City Road, for one; and there's the Surrey Gardens; and there's Rosherwich," he added, after a pause. (The Fisheries Exhibition, it may be said, was as yet unknown.)

" And you go there, often?"

" I've been to Rosherwich."

" Was it goot there—you laike it, eh?"

" Well," said Leander, " they tell me it's very gay in

the season. P'rhaps I went at the wrong time of the year for it."

"What you call wrong time for it?"

"Slack—nothing going on," he explained; "like it was when I went last Saturday."

"You went last Saturday? And you stay a long time?"

"I didn't stay no longer than I could help," Leander said. "All our party was glad to get away."

The foreigner had risen to go, when his eyes fell on the Venus in the corner.

"You did not stay long, and your party was glad to come away?" he repeated absently. "I am not surprised at that." He gave the hairdresser a long stare as he spoke. "No, I am not surprised. . . . You have a good taste, my friend; you laike the antique, do you not?" he broke off suddenly.

"Ah! you are looking at the Venus, sir," said Leander. "Yes, I'm very partial to it."

"It is a taste that costs," his customer said.

He looked back over his shoulder as he left the shop, and once more repeated softly, "Yes, it is a taste that costs."

"I suppose," Leander reflected as he went back, "it does strike people as queer, my keeping that statue there; but it's only for one evening."

The foreigner had scarcely left when an old gentleman, a regular customer, looked in, on his way from the City, and at once noticed the innovation. He was an old gentleman who had devoted much time and study to Art, in the intervals of business, and had developed critical powers of the highest order.

He walked straight up to the Venus, and stuck out his under lip. "Where did you get that thing?" he inquired. " Isn't this place of yours small enough, without lumbering it up with statuary out of the Euston Road ? "

" I didn't get it there," said Leander. " I—I thought it would be 'andy to 'ang the 'ats on."

" Dear, dear," said the old gentleman, " why do you people dabble in matters you don't understand ? Come here, Tweddle, and let me show you. Can't you *see* what a miserable sham the thing is—a cheap, tawdry imitation of the splendid classic type ? Why, by merely exhibiting such a thing, you're vitiating public taste, sir—corrupting it."

Leander did not quite follow this rebuke, which he thought was probably based upon the goddess's antecedents.

" Was she reelly as bad as that, sir ? " he said. " I wasn't aware so, or I shouldn't give any offence to customers by letting her stay here."

As he spoke he saw the indefinable indications in the statue's face which denoted that it was instinct once more with life and intelligence, and he was horrified at the thought that the latter part of the conversation might have been overheard.

" But I've always understood," he said, hastily, " that the party this represents was puffickly correct, however free some of the others might have been ; and I suppose that's the costume of the period she's in, and very becoming it is, I'm sure, though gone out since."

" Bah ! " said the old gentleman, " it's poor art. I'll show you *where* the thing is bad. I happen to understand something of these things. Just observe how the top of the head is out of drawing ; look at the lowness of the forehead, and the distance between the eyes ; all the canons of proportion ignored—absolutely ignored ! "

What further strictures this rash old gentleman was

preparing to pass upon the statue will never be known now, for Tweddle already thought he could discern a growing resentment in her face, under so much candour. He could not stand by and allow so excellent a customer to be crushed on the floor of his saloon, and he knew the Venus quite capable of this : was she not perpetually threatening such a penalty, on much slighter provocation ?

He rushed between the unconscious man and his fate. " I think you said your hair cut?" he said, and laid violent hands upon the critic, forced him protesting into a chair, throttled him with a towel, and effectually diverted his attention by a series of personal remarks upon the top of his head.

The victim, while he was being shampooed, showed at first an alarming tendency to revert to the subject of the goddess's defects, but Leander was able to keep him in check by well-timed jets of scalding water and ice-cold sprays, which he directed against his customer's exposed crown, until every idea, except impotent rage, was washed out of it, while a hard machine brush completed the subjugation.

Finally, the unfortunate old man staggered out of the shop, preserved by Leander's unremitting watchfulness from the wrath of the goddess. Yet, such is the ingratitude of human nature, that he left the place vowing to return no more. " I thought I'd got a *clown* behind me, sir !" he used to say afterwards, in describing it.

Before Leander could recover from the alarm he had been thrown into, another customer had entered ; a pale young man, with a glossy hat, a white satin necktie, and a rather decayed gardenia. He, too, was one of Tweddle's regular clients. What his occupation might be was a mystery, for he aimed at being considered a man of pleasure.

"I say, just shave me, will you?" he said, and threw himself languidly into a chair. "Fact is, Tweddle, I've been so doosid chippy for the last two days, I daren't touch a razor."

"Indeed, sir!" said Leander, with respectful sympathy.

"You see," explained the youth, "I've been playing the goat—the giddy goat. Know what that means?"

"I used to," said Leander; "I never touch alcoholic stimulants now, myself."

"Wish I didn't. I say, Tweddle, have you been to the Cosmopolitan lately?"

"I don't go to music-'alls now," said Leander; "I've give up all that now I'm keeping company."

"Well, you go and see the new ballet," the youth exhorted him earnestly; not that he cared whether the hairdresser went or not, but because he wanted to talk about the ballet to somebody.

"Ah!" observed Leander; "is that a good one they've got there now, sir?"

"Rather think so. Ballet called *Olympus*. There's a regular ripping little thing who comes on as one of Venus's doves." And the youth went on to intimate that the dove in question had shown signs of being struck by his powers of fascination. "I saw directly that I'd mashed her; she was gone, dead gone, sir; and—— I say, who's that in the corner over there—eh?"

He was staring intently into the pier-glass in front of him. "That?" said Leander, following his glance. "Oh! that's a statue I've bought. She—she brightens up the place a bit, don't she?"

"A statue, is it? Yes, of course; I knew it was a statue. Well, about that dove. I went round after it was all over, but couldn't see a sign of her; so——

"KEEP OFF! TELL HER TO DROP IT, TWEDDLE!"

[*Page* 87.

That's a queer sort of statue you've got there!" he broke off suddenly; and Leander distinctly saw the goddess shake her arm in fierce menace. "He's said something that's put her out," he concluded. "I wish I knew what it was."

"It's a classical statue, sir," he said, with what composure he might; "they're all made like that."

"Are they, by Jove? But, Tweddle, I say, it *moves:* it's shaking its fist like old Harry!"

"Oh, I think you're mistaken, sir, really! I don't perceive it myself."

"Don't perceive it? But, hang it, man, look—look in the glass! There! don't you see it does? Dash it! can't you *say* it does?"

"Flaw in the mirror, sir; when you move your 'ed, you do ketch that effect. I've observed it myself frequent. Chin cut, sir? My fault—my fault entirely," he admitted handsomely.

The young man was shaved by this time, and had risen to receive his hat and cane, when he gave a violent start as he passed the Aphrodite. "There!" he said, breathlessly, "look at that, Tweddle; she's going to punch my head! I suppose you'll tell me *that's* the glass?"

Leander trembled—this time for his own reputation; for the report that he kept a mysterious and pugnacious statue on the premises would not increase his custom. He must silence it, if possible. "I'm afraid it is, sir—in a way," he remarked, compassionately.

The young man turned paler still. "No!" he exclaimed. "You don't think it is, though? Don't you see anything yourself? I don't either, Tweddle; I was chaffing, that's all. I know I'm a wee bit off colour; but it's not so bad as that. Keep off! Tell her to drop it, Tweddle!"

87

For, as he spoke, the goddess had made a stride towards him. "Miserable one!" she cried, "you have mangled one of my birds. Hence, or I crush thee!"

"Tweddle! Tweddle!" cried the youth, taking refuge in the other shop, "don't let her come after me! What's she talking about, eh? You shouldn't have these things about; they're—they're not *right!*"

Leander shut the glass door and placed himself before it, while he tried to assume a concerned interest. "You take my advice, sir," he said; "you go home and keep steady."

"Is it that?" murmured the customer. "Great Scott! I must be bad!" and he went out into the street, shaking.

"I don't believe I shall ever see *him* again, either," thought Leander. "She'll drive 'em all away if she goes on like this." But here a sudden recollection struck him, and he slapped his thigh with glee. "Why, of course," he said, "that's it. I've downright disgusted her; it was me she was most put out with, and after this she'll leave me alone. Hooray! I'll shut up everything first and get rid of the boy, and then go in and see her, and get away to Matilda."

When the shop was secured for the night, he re-entered the saloon with a light step. "Well, mum," he began, "you've seen me at work, and you've thought better of what you were proposing, haven't you now?"

"Where is the wretched stripling who dared to slay my dove?" she cried. "Bring him to me!"

"What *are* you a-talking about now?" cried the bewildered Leander. "Who's been touching your birds? I wasn't aware you *kept* birds."

"Many birds are sacred to me—the silver swan, the fearless sparrow, and, chief of all, the coral-footed dove.

And one of these has that monster slain—his own mouth hath spoken it."

"Oh! is that all?" said Leander. "Why, he wasn't talking about a real dove; it was a ballet girl he meant. I can't explain the difference; but they *are* different. And it's all talk, too. I know him; *he's* harmless enough. And now, mum, to come to the point; you've now had the opportunity of forming some ideer of my calling. You've thought better of it, haven't you?"

"Better! ay, far better!" she cried, in a voice that thrilled with pride. "Leander, too modestly you have rated yourself, for surely you are great amongst the sons of men."

"*Me!*" he gasped, utterly overcome. "How do you make that out?"

"Do you not compel them to furnish sport for you? Have I not seen them come in, talking boldly and loud, and yet seat themselves submissively at a sign from you? And do you not swathe them in the garb of humiliation, and daub their countenances with whiteness, and threaten their bared throats with the gleaming knife, and grind their heads under the resistless wheel? Then, having in disdain granted them their worthless lives, you set them free; and they propitiate you with a gift, and depart trembling."

"Well, of all the topsy-turvy contrariness!" he protested. "You've got it *all* wrong; I declare you have! But I'll put you right, if it's possible to do it." And he launched into a lengthy explanation of the wonders she had seen, at the end of which he inquired, "*Now* do you understand I'm nobody in particular?"

"It may be so," she admitted; "but what of that? Ere this have I been wild with love for a herdsman on Phrygian hills. Aye, Adonis have I kissed in the oakwood, and bewailed his loss. And did not Selene descend to woo the neatherd Endymion? Wherefore, then, should I scorn thee? and what are the differences and degrees of mortals to such as I! Be bold; distrust your merits no longer, since I, who amongst the goddesses obtained the prize of beauty, have chosen you for my own."

"I don't care what prizes you won," he said, sulkily; "I'm not yours, and I don't intend to be, either." He was watching the clock impatiently all the while, for it was growing very near nine.

"It is vain to struggle," she said, "since not the gods themselves can resist Fate. We must yield, and contend not."

"You begin it, then," he said. "Give me my ring."

"The sole symbol of my power! the charm which has called me from my long sleep! Never!"

"Then," said Leander, knowing full well that his threat was an impossible one, "I shall place the matter in the hands of a respectable lawyer."

"I understand you not; but it is no matter. In time I shall prevail."

"Well, mum, you must come again another evening, if you've no objection," said Leander, rudely, "because I've got to go out just now."

"I will accompany you," she said.

Leander nearly danced with frenzy. Take the statue with him to meet his dear Matilda! He dared not. "You're very kind," he stammered, perspiring freely; "but I couldn't think of taking you out such a foggy evening."

"Have no cares for me," she answered; "we will go together. You shall explain to me the ways of this changed world."

"Catch *me!*" was Leander's elliptical comment to

himself; but he had to pretend a delighted acquiescence. "Well," he cried, "if I hadn't been thinking how lonely it would be going out alone! and now I shall have the honour of your company, mum. You wait a bit here, while I run upstairs and fetch my 'at."

But the perfidious man only waited until he was on the other side of the door, which led from the saloon to his staircase, to lock it after him, and slip out by the private door into the street.

"Now, my lady," he thought triumphantly, "you're safe for awhile, at all events. I've put up the shutters, and so you won't get out that way. And now for Tillie!"

TWO ARE COMPANY

VI.

"The shape
Which has made escape,
And before my countenance
Answers me glance for glance."

Mesmerism.

LEANDER hastened eagerly to his trysting-place. All these obstacles and difficulties had rendered his Matilda tenfold dearer and more precious to him ; and besides, it was more than a fortnight since he had last seen her. But he was troubled and anxious still at the recollection of the Greek statue shut up in his haircutting saloon. What would Matilda say if she knew about it ; and still worse, what might it not do if it knew about her? Matilda might decline to continue his acquaintance—for she was a very right-minded girl—unless Venus, like the jealous and vindictive heathen she had shown herself to be, were to crush her before she even had the opportunity.

"It's a mess," he thought disconsolately, "whatever way I look at it. But after to-night I won't meet Matilda any more while I've got that statue staying with me, or no one could tell the consequences." However, when he drew near the appointed spot, and saw the slender form which awaited him there by the railings, he forgot all but the present joy. Even the memory of the terrible divinity could not live in the wholesome presence of the girl he had the sense to truly and honestly love.

Matilda Collum was straight and slim, though not tall; she had a neat little head of light brown hair, which curled round her temples in soft rings; her complexion was healthily pale, with the slightest tinge of delicate pink in it; she had a round but decided chin, and her grey eyes were large and innocently severe, except on the rare occasions when she laughed, and then their expression was almost childlike in its gaiety.

Generally, and especially in business hours, her pretty face was calm and slightly haughty, and rash male customers who attempted to make the choice of a "button-hole" an excuse for flirtation were not encouraged to persevere. She was seldom demonstrative to Leander—it was not her way—but she accepted his effusive affection very contentedly, and, indeed, returned it more heartily than her principles allowed her to admit; for she secretly admired his spirit and fluency, and, as is often the case in her class of life, had no idea that she was essentially her lover's superior.

After the first greetings, they walked slowly round the square together, his arm around her waist. Neither said very much for some minutes, but Leander was wildly, foolishly happy, and there was no severity in Matilda's eyes when they shone in the lamp-light.

"Well," he said, at last, "and so I've actially got you safe back again, my dear, darling Tillie! It seems like a long eternity since last we met. I've been so beastly miserable, Matilda!"

"You do seem to have got thinner in the face, Leander dear," said Matilda, compassionately. "What *have* you been doing while I've been away?"

"Only wishing my dearest girl back, that's all *I've* been doing."

"What! haven't you given yourself any enjoyment at all—not gone out anywhere all the time?"

"Not once—leastwise, that is to say——" A guilty memory of Rosherwich made him bungle here.

"Why, of course I didn't expect you to stop indoors all the time," said Matilda, noticing the amendment, "so long as you never went where you wouldn't take me."

Oh, conscience, conscience! But Rosherwich didn't count—it was outside the radius; and besides, he *hadn't* enjoyed himself.

"Well," he said, "I did go out one evening, to hear a lecture on Astronomy at the Town Hall, in the Gray's Inn Road; but then I had the ticket given me by a customer, and I reely was surprised to find how regular the stars was in their habits, comets and all. But my 'Tilda is the only star of the evening for me, to-night. I don't want to talk about anything else."

The diversion was successful, and Matilda asked no more inconvenient questions. Presently she happened to cough slightly, and he touched accusingly the light summer cloak she was wearing.

"You're not dressed warm enough for a night like this," he said, with a lover's concern. "Haven't you got anything thicker to put on than that?"

"I haven't bought my winter things yet," said Matilda; "it was so mild, that I thought I'd wait till I could afford it better. But I've chosen the very thing I mean to buy. You know Mrs. Twilling's, at the top of the Row, the corner shop? Well, in the window there's a perfectly lovely long cloak, all lined with squirrel's fur, and with those nice oxidized silver fastenings. A cloak like that lasts ever so long, and will always look neat and quiet;

and any one can wear it without being stared after; so I mean to buy it as soon as it turns really cold."

"Ah!" said he, "I can't have you ketching cold, you know; it ain't summer any longer, and I—I've been thinking we must give up our evening strolls together for the present."

"When you've just been saying how miserable you've been without them. Oh, Leander!"

"Without *you*," he amended lamely. "I shall see you at aunt's, of course; only we'd better suspend the walks while the nights are so raw. And, oh, Tillie, ere long you will be mine, my little wife! Only to think of you keeping the books for me with your own pretty little fingers, and sending out the bills! (not that I give much credit). Ah, what a blissful dream it sounds! Does it to you, Matilda?"

"I'm not sure that you keep your books the same way as we do," she replied demurely; "but I dare say"—(and this was a great concession for Matilda)—"I dare say we shall suit one another."

"Suit one another!" he cried. "Ah! we shall be inseparable as a brush and comb, Tillie, if you'll excuse so puffessional a stimulus. And what a future lies before me! If I can only succeed in introducing some of my inventions to public notice, we may rise, Tilly, 'like an exclamation,' as the poet says. I believe my new nasal splint has only to be known to become universally worn; and I've been thinking out a little machine lately for imparting a patrician arch to the flattest foot, that ought to have an extensive run. I almost wish you weren't so pretty, Tillie. I've studied you careful, and I'm bound to say, as it is there really isn't room for any improvement I could suggest. Nature's beaten me there, and I'm not too proud to own it."

"Would you rather there *was* room!" inquired Matilda.

"From a puffessional point of view, it would have inspired me," he said. "It would have suggested ideers, and I shouldn't have loved you less, not if you hadn't had a tooth in your mouth nor a hair on your head; you would still be my beautiful Tillie."

"I would rather be as I am, thank you," said Matilda, to whom this fancy sketch did not appeal. "And now, let's talk about something else. Do you know that mamma is coming up to town at the end of the week on purpose to see you?"

"No," said Leander, "I—I didn't."

"Yes, she's taken the whole of your aunt's first floor for a week. (You know, she knew Miss Tweddle when she was younger, and that was how I came to lodge there, and to meet you.) Do you remember that Sunday afternoon you came to tea, and your aunt invited me in, because she thought I must be feeling so dull, all alone?"

"Ah, I should think I did! Do you remember I helped to toast the crumpets? What a halcyon evening that was, Matilda!"

"Was it?" she said. "I don't remember the weather exactly; but it was nice indoors."

"But, I say, Tillie, my own," he said, somewhat anxiously, "how does your ma like your being engaged to me?"

"Well, I don't think she does like it quite," said Matilda. "She says she will reserve her consent till she sees whether you are worthy; but directly she sees you, Leander, her objections will vanish."

"She has got objections, then? What to?"

"Mother always wanted me to keep my affections out

of trade," said Matilda. "You see, she never can forget what poor papa was."

"And what was your poor papa?" asked Leander.

"Didn't you know? He was a dentist, and that makes mamma so very particular, you see."

"But, hang it, Matilda! you're employed in a flower-shop, you know."

"Yes, but mamma never really approved of it; only she had to give way because she couldn't afford to keep me at home, and I scorned to go out as a governess. Never mind, Leander; when she comes to know you and hear your conversation, she will relent; her pride will melt."

"But suppose it keeps solid; what will you do, Matilda?"

"I am independent, Leander; and though I would prefer to marry with mamma's approval, I shouldn't feel bound to wait for it. So long as you are all I think you are, I shouldn't allow any one to dictate to me."

"Bless you for those words, my angelic girl!" he said, and hugged her close to his breast. "Now I can beard your ma with a light 'art. Oh, Matilda! you can form no ideer how I worship you. Nothing shall ever come betwixt us two, shall it?"

"Nothing, as far as I am concerned, Leander," she replied. "What's the matter?"

He had given a furtive glance behind him after the last remarks, and his embrace suddenly relaxed, until his arm was withdrawn altogether.

"Nothing is the matter, Matilda," he said. "Doesn't the moon look red through the fog?"

"Is that why you took away your arm?" she inquired.

"Yes—that is, no. It occurred to me I was

rendering you too conspicuous; we don't want to go about advertising ourselves, you know."

"But who is there here to notice?" asked Matilda.

"Nobody," he said; "oh, nobody! but we mustn't get into the *way* of it;" and he cast another furtive rearward look. In the full flow of his raptures the miserable hairdresser had seen a sight which had frozen his very marrow—a tall form, in flowing drapery, gliding up behind with a tigress-like stealth. The statue had broken out, in spite of all his precautions! Venus, jealous and exacting, was near enough to overhear every word, and he could scarcely hope she had escaped seeing the arm he had thrown round Matilda's waist.

"You were going to tell me how you worshipped me," said Matilda.

"I didn't say |*worship*," he protested; "it—it's only images and such that expect that. But I can tell you there's very few brothers feel to you as I feel."

"*Brothers*, Leander!" exclaimed Matilda, and walked farther apart from him.

"Yes," he said. "After all, what tie's closer than a brother? A uncle's all very well, and similarly a cousin; but they can't feel like a brother does, for brothers they are not."

"I should have thought there were ties still closer," said Matilda; "you seemed to think so too, once."

"Oh, ah! *that!*" he said. (Every frigid word gave him a pang to utter; but it was all for Matilda's sake.) "There's time enough to think of that, my girl; we mustn't be in a hurry."

"I'm *not* in a hurry," said Matilda.

"That's the proper way to look at it," said he; "and meanwhile I haven't got a sister I'm fonder of than I am of you."

"If you've nothing more to say than that, we had better part," she remarked; and he caught at the suggestion with obvious relief. He had been in an agony of terror, lest, even in the gathering fog, she should detect that they were watched; and then, too, it was better to part with her under a temporary misconception than part with her altogether.

"Well," he said, "I mustn't keep you out any longer, with that cold."

"You are very ready to get rid of me," said poor Matilda.

"The real truth is," he answered, simulating a yawn with a heavy heart; "I am most uncommon sleepy to-night, and all this standing about is too much for me. So good-bye, and take care of yourself!"

"I needn't say that to you," she said; "but I won't keep you up a minute longer. I wonder you troubled to come out at all."

"Oh," he said, carefully keeping as much in front of the statue as he could, "it's no trouble; but you'll excuse me seeing you to the door this evening?"

"Oh, certainly," said Matilda, biting her lip. She touched his hand with the ends of her fingers, and hurried away without turning her head.

When she was out of sight, Leander faced round to the irrepressible goddess. He was in a white rage; but terror and caution made him suppress it to some extent.

"So here you are again!" he said.

"Why did you not wait for me?" she answered. "I remained long for you; you came not, and I followed."

"I see you did," said the aggrieved Leander; "I can't say I like being spied upon. If you're a goddess, act as such!"

"IT IS A MISERABLE THING," HE WAS THINKING, "FOR A MAN
. . . TO HAVE A FEMALE STATUE TROTTING AFTER HIM
LIKE A GREAT DORG." {*Page* 105.

"What! you dare to upbraid me?" she cried. "Beware, or I—— "

"I know," said Leander, flinching from her. "Don't do that; I only made a remark."

"I have the right to follow you; I choose to do so."

"If you must, you must," he groaned; "but it does seem hard that I mayn't slip out for a few minutes' talk with my only sister."

"You said you were going to run for business, and you told me you had three sisters."

"So I have; but only one *youngest* one."

"And why did they not all come to talk with you?"

"I suppose because the other two stayed at home," rejoined Leander, sulkily.

"I know not why, but I doubt you; that one who came, she is not like you!"

"No," said Leander, with a great show of candour, "that's what every one says; all our family are like that; we are like in a way, because we're all of us so different. You can tell us anywhere just by the difference. My father and mother were both very unlike: I suppose we take after them."

The goddess seemed satisfied with this explanation. "And now that I have regained you, let us return to your abode," she said; and Leander walked back by her side, a prey to rage and humiliation.

"It is a miserable thing," he was thinking, "for a man in my rank of life to have a female statue trotting after him like a great dorg. I'm d——d if I put up with it! Suppose we happen on somebody as knows me!"

Fortunately, at that time of night Bloomsbury Square is not much frequented; the increasing fog prevented the apparition of a female in classical garments from attracting the notice to which it might otherwise have been exposed, and they reached the shop without any disagreeable encounter.

"She shan't stop in the saloon," he determined; "I've had enough of that! If you've no objections," he said, with a mixture of deference and dictation, "I shall be obliged if you'd settle yourself in the little shrine in the upstairs room before proceeding to evaporate out of your statue; it would be more agreeable to my feelings."

"Ah!" she said, smiling, "you would have me nearer you? Your stubborn heart is yielding; a little while, and you will own the power of Aphrodite!"

"Now, don't you go deceiving yourself with any such ideers," said the hairdresser, irritably. "I shan't do no such thing, so you needn't think it. And, to come to the point, how long do you mean to carry on this little game?"

"Game?" repeated the goddess, absently.

"How long are you going to foller me about in this ridiclous way?"

"Till you submit, and profess your willingness to redeem your promise."

"Oh, and you're coming every evening till then, are you?"

"At nightfall of each day I have power to revisit you."

"Well, come then!" he said, with a fling of impatient anger. "I tell you beforehand that you won't get anything by it. Not if you was to come and bring a whole stonemason's yard of sculptures along with you, you wouldn't! You ought to know better than to come pestering a respectable tradesman in this bold-faced manner!"

She smiled with a languid contemptuous tolerance, which maddened Leander.

"Rave on," she said. "Truly, you are a sorry prize for such as I to stoop to win; yet I will it, nor shall you escape me. There will come a day when, forsaken by all you hold dear on earth, despised, ruined, distracted, you will pray eagerly for the haven of refuge to which I alone can guide you. Take heed, lest your conduct now be remembered then! I have spoken."

They were indeed her last words that evening, and they impressed the hairdresser, in spite of himself. Custom habituates the mind to any marvel, and already he had overcome his first horror at the periodical awakenings of the statue, and surprise was swallowed up by exasperation; now, however, he quailed under her dark threats. Could it ever really come to pass that he would sue to this stone to hide him in the realms of the supernatural?

"I know this," he told himself, "if it once gets about that there's a hairdresser to be seen in Bloomsbury chivied about after dark by a classical statue, I shan't dare to show my face. Yet I don't know how I'm to prevent her coming out after me, at all events now and then. If she was only a little more like other people, I shouldn't mind so much; but it's more than I can bear to have to go about with a *tablow vivant* or a *pose plastique* on my arm!"

All at once he started to his feet. "I've got it!" he cried, and went downstairs to his laboratory, to reappear with some camel-hair brushes, grease-paints, and a selection from his less important discoveries in the science of cosmetics; namely, an "eyebrow accentuator," a vase of "Tweddle's Cream of Carnations" and "Blondinette Bloom," a china box of "Conserve of Coral" for the lips, and one of his most expensive *chevelures*.

He was trembling as he arranged them upon his

table; not that he was aware of the enormity of the act he contemplated, but he was afraid the goddess might revisit the marble while he was engaged upon it.

He furnished the blank eye-sockets with a pair of eyes, which, if not exactly artistic, at least supplied a want; he pencilled the eyebrows, laid on several coats of the " Bloom," which he suffused cunningly with a tinge of carnation, and stained the pouting lips with his " Conserve of Coral."

So far, perhaps, he had not violated the canons of art, and may even have restored to the image something of its pristine hues; but his next addition was one the vandalism of which admits of no possible defence, and when he deftly fitted the coiffure of light closely-curled hair upon the noble classical head, even Leander felt dimly that something was wrong !

" I don't know how it is," he pondered; " she looks more natural, but not half so respectable. However, when she's got something on to cover the marble, there won't be anything much to notice about her. I'll buy a cloak for her the first thing to-morrow morning. Matilda was saying something about a shop near here where I could get that. And then, if this Venus must come following me about, she'll look less outlandish at any rate, and that's something ! "

A FURTHER PREDICAMENT

II

VII.

"So long as the world contains us both,
    Me the loving and you the loth,
    While the one eludes, must the other pursue."

Browning.

IMMEDIATELY after breakfast the next day, Leander went out and paid a visit to Miss Twilling's, bringing away with him a hooded cloak of the precise kind he remembered Matilda to have described as unlikely to render its owner conspicuous. With this garment he succeeded in disguising the statue to such a degree, that it was far less likely than before that the goddess's appearance in public would excite any particular curiosity—a result which somewhat relieved his anxiety as to her future proceedings.

But all that day his thoughts were busy with Matilda. He must, he feared, have deeply offended her by his abrupt change on the previous night ; and now he could not expect to meet her again for days, and would not know how to explain his conduct if he did meet her.

If he could only dare to tell her everything ; but from such a course he shrank. Matilda would not only be extremely indignant (though, in very truth, he had done nothing positively wrong as yet), but, with her strict notions and well-regulated principles, she would assuredly recoil from a lover who had brought himself into a predicament so hideous. He would tell her all when, or if, he succeeded in extricating himself.

But he was to learn the nature of Matilda's sentiments sooner than he expected. It was growing dusk, and he was unpacking a parcel of goods in his front shop—for his saloon happened to be empty just then—when the outer door swung back, and a slight girlish figure entered, after a pause of indecision on the threshold. It was Matilda.

Had she come to break it off—to reproach him? He was prepared for no less; she had never paid him a visit like this alone before; and some doubts of the propriety of the thing seemed to be troubling her now, for she did not speak.

"Matilda," he faltered, "don't tell me you have come in a spirit of unpleasantness, for I can't bear it."

"Don't you deserve that I should?" she said, but not angrily. "You know, you were very strange in behaving as you did last night. I couldn't tell what to make of it."

"I know," he said confusedly; "it was something come over me, all of a sudden like. I can't understand what made me like that; but, oh, Tillie, my dearest love, my 'art was busting with adoration all the time! The circumstances was highly peculiar; but I don't know that I could explain them."

"You needn't, Leander; I have found you out." She said this with a strange significance.

"What!" he almost shrieked. "You don't mean it, Matilda! Tell me, quick! has the discovery changed your feelings towards me? Has it?"

"Yes," she said softly. "I—I think it has; but you ought not to have done it, Leander."

"I know," he groaned. "I was a fool, Tillie; a fool! But I may get out of it yet," he added. "I can get her to let me off. I must—I will!"

Matilda opened her eyes. "But, Leander dear, listen; don't be so hasty. I never said I *wanted* her to let you off, did I?

He looked at her in a dazed manner. "I rather thought," he said slowly, "that it might have put you out a little. I see I was mistook."

"You might have known that I should be more pleased than angry, I should think," said Matilda.

"More pleased than—— I might have known!" exclaimed the bewildered man. "Oh, you can't reely be taking it as cool as this! Will you kindly inform me *what* it is you're alludin' to in this way?"

"What is the use of pretending? You know I know. And it *is* colder, much colder, this morning. I felt it directly I got up."

"Quite a change in the weather, I'm sure," he said mechanically; "it feels like a frost coming on." ("Has Matilda looked in to tell me the weather's changed?" he was wondering within himself. "Either I'm mad, or Matilda is.")

"You dear old goose!" said Matilda, with an unusual effusiveness; "you shan't tease me like this! Do you think I've no eyes and no feelings? Any girl, I don't care how proud or offended, would come round on such proof of devotedness as I've had this evening. When I saw it gone, I felt I must come straight in and thank you, and tell you I shouldn't think any more of last night. I couldn't stop myself."

"When you saw *what* gone?" cried the hairdresser, rubbing up his hair.

"The cloak," said Matilda; and then, as she saw his

expression, her own changed. " Leander Tweddle," she asked, in a dry hard voice, "have I been making a wretched fool of myself? *Didn't* you buy that cloak ?"

He understood at last. He had gone to Miss Twilling's chiefly because he was in a hurry and it was close by, and he knew nowhere else where he could be sure of getting what he required. Now, by some supreme stroke of the ill-luck which seemed to be pursuing him of late, he had unwittingly purchased the identical garment on which Matilda had fixed her affections ! How was he to notice that they took it out of the window for him ?

All this flashed across him as he replied, " Yes, yes, Tillie, I did buy a cloak there ; but are you sure it was the same you told me about ?"

" Do you think a woman doesn't know the look of a thing like that, when it's taken her fancy ?" said Matilda. " Why, I could tell you every clasp and tassel on that cloak ; it wasn't one you'd see every day, and I knew it was gone the moment I passed the window. It quite upset me, for I'd set my heart on it so ; and I ran in to Miss Twilling, and asked her what had become of it ; and when she said she'd sold it that morning, I thought I should have fainted. You see, it never struck me that it could be you ; for how could I dream that you'd be clever enough to go and choose the very one ? Leander, it *was* clever of you !"

" Yes," he said, with a bitter rail against himself, " I'm a clever chap, I am ! But how did you find out ?"

" Oh, I made Miss Twilling (I often get little things there), I made her describe who she sold it to, and she said she thought it was to a gentleman in the haircutting persuasion who lived near ; and then, of course, I guessed who bought it."

"Tillie," gasped Leander, "I—I didn't *mean* you to guess ; the purpose for which I require that cloak is my secret."

"Oh, you silly man, when I've guessed it ! And I take it just as kind of you as if it was to be all a surprise. I was wishing as I came along I could afford to buy it at once, it struck so cold coming out of our place ; and you had actually bought it for me all the time ! Thank you ever so much, Leander dear !"

He had only to accept the position ; and he did. " I'm glad you're pleased," he said ; " I intended it as a surprise."

"And I am surprised," said Matilda ; " because, do you know, last night, when I went home, I was feeling very cross with you. I kept thinking that perhaps you didn't care for me any more, and were trying to break it off ; and, oh, all sorts of horrid things I kept thinking ! And aunt gave me a message for you this morning, and I was so out of temper I wouldn't leave it. And now to find you've been so kind !"

She stretched out her hand to him across the counter, and he took and held it tight ; he had never seen her looking sweeter, nor felt that she was half so dear to him. After all, his blunder had brought them together again, and he was grateful to it.

At last Matilda said, " You were quite right about this wrapper, Leander ; it's not half warm enough for a night like this. I'm really afraid to go home in it."

He knew well enough what she intended him to do ; but just then he dared not appear to understand. " It isn't far, only to Millman Street," he said ; " and you must walk fast, Tillie. I wish I could leave the shop and come too."

" You want me to ask you downright," she said

pouting. "You men can't even be kind prettily. Don't you want to see how I look in your cloak, Leander?"

What could he say after that? He must run upstairs, deprive the goddess of her mantle, and hand it over to Matilda. She had evidently made up her mind to have that particular cloak, and he must buy the statue another. It would be expensive; but there was no help for it.

"Certainly," he said, "you shall have it now, dearest, if you'd like to. I'll run up and fetch it down, if you'll wait."

He rushed upstairs, two steps at a time, and, flinging open the door of a cupboard, began desperately to uncloak his Aphrodite. She was lifeless still, which he considered fortunate.

But the goddess seemed to have a natural propensity to retain any form of portable property. One of her arms was so placed that, tug and stretch as he would, Leander could not get the cloak from her shoulders, and his efforts only broke one of the oxidized silver fastenings, and tore part of the squirrel's-fur lining.

It was useless, and with a damp forehead he came down again to his expectant *fiancée*.

"Why, you haven't got it, after all!" she cried, her face falling.

"Tillie, my own dear girl," he said, "I'm uncommon sorry, upon my soul I am, but you can't have that cloak this evening."

"But why, Leander, why?"

"Because one of the clasps is broke. It must be sent back to be repaired."

"I don't mind that. Let me have it just as it is."

"And the lining's torn. No, Matilda, I shan't make you a present of a damaged article. I shall send it back.

They must change it for me." (" Then," he thought, " I can buy my Matilda another.")

" I don't care for any other but that," she said; "and you can't match it."

" Oh, lor !" he thought, "and she knows every inch of it. The goddess must give it up; it'll be all the same to *her*. Very well then, dearest, you *shall* have that, but not till it's done up. I must have my way in this; and as soon as ever I can, I'll bring it round."

" Leander, could you bring it me by Sunday," she said eagerly, " when you come ?"

" Why Sunday ?" he asked.

" Because—oh, that was the message your aunt asked me to bring you; it was in a note, but I've lost it. She told me what was inside though, and it's this. Will you give her the pleasure of your company at her mid-day dinner at two o'clock, to be introduced to mamma ? And she said you were to be sure and not forget her ring."

He tottered for a moment. The ring ! Yes, there was that to be got off, too, besides the cloak.

" Haven't you got the ring from Vidler's yet ?" she said. " He's had it such a time."

He had told her where he had left it for alterations. " Yes," he said, " he has had it a time. It's disgraceful the way that old Vidler potters and potters. I shall go round and 'urry him up. I won't stand it any longer."

Here a customer came in, and Matilda slipped away with a hurried good-bye.

" I've got till Sunday to get straight," the hairdresser thought, as he attended on the new comer, "the best part of a week; surely I can talk that Venus over by that time."

When he was alone he went up to see her, without losing a moment. He must have left the door unlocked in his haste, for she was standing before the low chimney-glass, regarding herself intently. As he came in she turned.

"Who has done all this?" she demanded. "Tell me, was it you?"

"I did take the liberty, mum," he faltered guiltily.

"You have done well," she said graciously. "With reverent and loving care have you imparted hues as of life to these cheeks, and decked my image in robes of costly skins."

"Don't name it, mum," he said.

"But what are these?" she continued, raising a hand to the light ringlets on her brow. "I like them not—they are unseemly. The waving lines, parted by the bold chisel of a Grecian sculptor, resemble my ambrosial tresses more nearly than this abomination."

"You may go all over London," said Leander, "and you won't find a coiffure, though I say it, to set closer and defy detection more naturally than the one you've got on; selected from the best imported foreign hair in the market, I do assure you."

"I accept the offering for the spirit in which it was presented, though I approve it not otherwise."

"You'll find it wear very comfortable," said Leander; "but that cloak, now I come to see it on, it reely is most unworthy of you, a very inferior piece of goods, and, if you'll allow me, I'll change it," and he gently extended his hand to draw it off.

"Touch it not," said the goddess; "for, having once been placed upon my effigy, it is consecrated to my service."

"For mercy's sake, let me get another one—one with more style about it," he entreated; "my credit hangs on it!"

SHE WAS STANDING BEFORE THE LOW CHIMNEY-GLASS, REGARDING
HERSELF INTENTLY.   [*Page* 118.

"I am content," she said, "more than content. No more words—I retain it. And you have pleased me by this conduct, my hairdresser. Unknown it may be, even to yourself, your heart is warming in the sunshine of my favour; you are coy and wayward, but you are yielding. Though pent in this form, carved by a mortal hand, I shall prevail in the end. I shall have you for my own."

He rumpled his hair wildly, "'Orrid obstinate these goddesses are," he thought. "What am I to say to Matilda now? If I could only find a way of getting this statue shut up somewhere where she couldn't come and bother me, I'd take my chance of the rest. I can't go on with this sort of thing every evening. I'm sick and tired of it."

Then something occurred to him. "Could I delude her into it?" he asked himself. "She's soft enough in some things, and, for all she's a goddess, she don't seem up to our London ways yet. I'll have a try, anyway."

So he began: "Didn't I understand you to observe, mum, some time back, that the pidgings and sparrers were your birds?"

"They are mine," she said—"or they were mine in days that are past."

"Well," he said, "there's a place close by, with railings in front of it, and steps and pillars as you go in, and if you like to go and look in the yard there you'll find pidgings enough to set you up again. I shouldn't wonder if they've been keeping them for you all this time."

"They shall not lose by it," she said. "Go thither, and bring me my birds."

"I think," he said, "it would be better if you'd go yourself; they don't know me at the British Museum. But if you was to go to the beadle at the lodge and demand them, I've no doubt you'd be attended to; and you'll see some parties at the gates in long coats and black cloth 'elmets, which if you ask them to ketch you a few sparrers, they'll probably be most happy to oblige."

"My beloved birds!" she said. "I have been absent from them so long. Yes, I will go. Tell me where."

He got his hat, and went with her to a corner of Bloomsbury Square, from which they could see the railings fronting the Museum in the steel-tinted haze of electric light.

"That's the place," he said. "Keeps its own moonshine, you see. Go straight in, and tell 'em you're come to fetch your doves."

"I will do so," she said, and strode off in imperious majesty.

He looked after her with an irrepressible chuckle.

"If she ain't locked up soon, I don't know myself," he said, and went back to his establishment.

He had only just dismissed his apprentice and secured the shop for the night, when he heard the well-known tread up the staircase. "Back again! I don't have any luck," he muttered; and with reason, for the statue, wearing an expression of cold displeasure, advanced into his room. He felt a certain sense of guilt as he saw her.

"Got the birds?" he inquired, with a nervous familiarity, "or couldn't you bring yourself to ask for them?"

"You have misled me," she said. "My birds are not there. I came to gates in front of a stately pile—doubtless erected to some god; at the entrance stood a priest, burly and strong, with gold-embroidered garments—— "

("The beadle, I suppose," commented Leander.)

"I passed him unseen, and roamed unhindered over

the courtyard. It was bare, save for one or two
worshippers who crossed it. Presently a winged thing
fluttered down to my feet. But though a dove indeed,
it was no bird of mine—it knew me not. And it was
draggled, begrimed, uncleanly, as never were the doves
of Aphrodite. And the sparrows (for these, too, did I
see), they were worse. I motioned them from me with
loathing. I renounced them all. Thus, Leander, have
I fared in following your counsels!"

"Well, it ain't my fault," he said; "it's the London
soot makes them like that. There's some at the Guild-
hall: perhaps they're cleaner."

"No," she said, vehemently; "I will seek no further.
This is a city of darkness and mire. I am in a land, an
age, which know me not: this much have I learnt already.
The world was fairer and brighter of old!"

"You see," said Leander, "if you only go about at
night, you can't expect sunshine! But I'm told there's
cleaner and brighter places to be seen abroad—if you
cared to go there?" he insinuated.

"To one place only, to my Cyprian caves, will I go,"
she declared, "and with you!"

"We'll talk about that some other time," he answered,
soothingly. "Lady Venus, look here, don't you think
you've kept that ring long enough? I've asked you
civilly enough, goodness knows, to 'and it over, times
without number. I ask you once more to act fair. You
know it came to you quite accidental, and yet you want
to take advantage of it like this. It ain't right!"

She met this with her usual scornful smile. "Listen,
Leander," she said. "Once before—how long since I
know not—a mortal, in sport or accident, placed his ring
as you have done upon the finger of a statue erected to
me. I claimed fulfilment of the pledge then, as now;

but a force I could not withstand was invoked against me, and I was made to give up the ring, and with it the power and rights I strove to exert. But I will not again be thwarted : no force, no being shall snatch you from me ; so be not deceived. Submit, ere you excite my fierce displeasure ; submit now, since in the end submit you must ! "

There was a dreadful force in the sonorous tones which made him shiver ; a rigid inflexible will lurked in this form, with all its subtle curves and feminine grace. If goddesses really retained any power in these days, there could be no doubt that she would use hers to the full.

Yet he still struggled. " I can't make you give up the ring," he said ; " but no more you can't make me leave my—my establishment, and go away underground with you. I'm an Englishman, I am, and Englishmen are free, mum ; p'r'aps you wasn't aware of that ? I've got a will of my own, and so you'll find it ! "

" Poor worm ! " she said pityingly (and the hairdresser hated to be addressed as a poor worm), " why oppose thy weak will to mine ? Why enlist my pride against thyself ; for what hast thou of thine own to render thy conquest desirable ? Thou art bent upon defiance, it seems. I leave thee to reflect if such a combat can be equal. Farewell ; and at my next coming let me find a change ! "

And the spirit of the goddess fled, as before, to the mysterious realms from which she had been so incautiously evoked, leaving Leander almost frantic with rage, superstitious terror, and baffled purposes.

" I must get the ring off," he muttered, " *and* the cloak, somehow. Oh ! if I could only find out how—— There was that other chap—*he* got off ; she said as much. If I could get out how he managed it, why couldn't I do the same? But who's to tell me? She won't—not if she knows it! I wonder if it's in any history. Old Freemoult would know it if it was—he's such a scholar. Why, he gave me a name for that 'airwash without having to think twice over it! I'll try and pump old Freemoult. I'll do it to-morrow, too. I'll see if I'm to be domineered over by a image out of a tea-garden. Eh? I—I don't care if she *did* hear me!"

So Leander went to his troubled pillow, full of this new resolution, which seemed to promise a way of escape.

BETWEEN THE DEVIL AND
THE DEEP SEA

VIII.

" Some, when they take *Revenge*, are Desirous the party should
know whence it cometh : This is the more Generous."—BACON.

IN the Tottenham Court Road was a certain Commercial
Dining-room, where Leander occasionally took his evening
meal, after the conclusion of his day's work, and where
Mr. Freemoult was accustomed to take his supper, on
leaving the British Museum Library.

To this eating-house Leander repaired the very next
evening, urged by a consuming desire to learn the full
particulars of the adventure which his prototype in misfortune had met with.

It was an unpretending little place, with the bill of
fare wafered to the door, and red curtains in the windows,
setting off a display of joints, cauliflowers, and red
herrings. He passed through into a long, low room,
with dark-brown grained walls, partitioned off in the
usual manner ; and taking a seat in a box facing the
door, he ordered dinner from one of the shirtsleeved
attendants.

The first glance had told him that the man he wished
to see was not there, but he knew he must come in before
long ; and, in fact, before Leander's food could be brought,
the old scholar made his appearance.

He was hardly a man of attractive exterior, being of a yellow complexion, with a stubbly chin, and lank iron-grey locks. He wore a tall and superannuated hat with a staring nap, and the pockets of his baggy coat bulged with documents. Altogether he did not seem exactly the person to be an authority on the subject of Venus.

But, as the hairdresser was aware, he had the reputation of being a mine of curious and out-of-the-way information, though few thought it worth their while to work him. He gained a living, however, by hackwork of various descriptions, and was in slightly better circumstances than he allowed to appear.

As he passed slowly along the central passage, in his usual state of abstraction, Leander touched him eagerly on the sleeve. "Come in 'ere, Mr. Freemoult, sir," he said; "there's room in this box."

"It's the barber, is it?" said the old man. "What do you want me to eat with you for, eh?"

"Why, for the pleasure of your company, sir, of course," said Leander, politely.

"Well," said the old gentleman, sitting down, while documents bristled out of him in all directions, "there are not many who would say that—not many now."

"Don't you say so, Mr. Freemoult, sir. I'm sure it's a benefit, if only for your conversation. I often say, 'I never meet Mr. Freemoult without I learn somethink;' I do indeed."

"Then we must have met less often than I had imagined."

"Now, you're too modest, sir; you reelly are—a scholar like you, too! Talking of scholarship, you'll be gratified to hear that that title you were good enough to suggest for the 'Regenerator' is having a quite surprising success. I disposed of five bottles over the counter only yesterday." ("These old scholars," was his wily reflection, "like being flattered up.")

"Does that mean you've another beastly bottle you want me to stand godfather to?" growled the ungrateful old gentleman.

"Oh no, indeed, sir! It's only—— But p'r'aps you'll allow me previously the honour of sending out for whatever beverage you was thinking of washing down your boiled beef with, sir."

"Do you know who I am?" Mr. Freemoult burst out. "I'm a scholar, and gentleman enough still to drink at my own expense!"

"I intended no offence, I'm sure, sir; it was only meant in a friendly way."

"That is the offence, sir; that *is* the offence! But, there, we'll say no more about it; you can't help your profession, and I can't help my prejudices. What was it you wanted to ask me?"

"Well," said Leander, "I was desirous of getting some information respecting—ahem—a party by the name of (if I've caught the foreign pronounciation) Haphrodite, otherwise known as Venus. Do you happen to have heard tell of her?"

"Have I had a classical education, sir, or haven't I? Heard of her? Of course I have. But why, in the name of Mythology, any hairdresser living should trouble his head about Aphrodite, passes my comprehension. Leave her alone, sir!"

"It's her who won't leave *me* alone!" thought Leander; but he did not say so. "I've a very particular reason for wishing to know; and I'm sure if you could tell me all you'd heard about her, I'd take it very kind of you."

"Want to pick my brains; well, you wouldn't be the

first. But I am here, sir, to rest my brain and refresh my body, not to deliver peripatetic lectures to hairdressers on Grecian mythology."

"Well," said Leander, "I never meant you to give your information peripatetic; I'm willing to go as far as half a crown."

"Conf—— But, there, what's the good of being angry with you? Is this the sort of thing you want for your half-crown?—Aphrodite, a later form of the Assyrian Astarte; the daughter, according to some theogonies, of Zeus and Dione; others have it that she was the offspring of the foam of the sea, which gathered round the fragments of the mutilated Uranos——"

"That don't seem so likely, do it, sir?" said Leander.

"If you are going to crop in with idiotic remarks, I shall confine myself to my supper."

"Don't stop, Mr. Freemoult, sir; it's most instructive. I'm attending."

But the old gentleman, after a manner he had, was sunk in a dreamy abstraction for the moment, in which he apparently lost the thread, as he resumed, "Whereupon Zeus, to punish her, gave her in wedlock to his deformed son, Hephæstus."

"She never mentioned him to *me*," thought Leander; "but I suppose she's a widow goddess by this time; I'm sure I *hope* so."

"Whom," Mr. Freemoult was saying, "she deceived upon several occasions, notably in the case of——" And here he launched into a scandalous chronicle, which determined Leander more than ever that Matilda must never know he had entertained a personage with such a past.

"Angered by her indiscretions, Zeus inspired her with love for a mortal man."

"Poor devil!" said Leander, involuntarily. "And what became of *him*, sir?"

"There were several thus distinguished; amongst others, Anchises, Adonis, and Cinyras. Of these, the first was struck by lightning; the second slain by a wild boar; and the third is reputed to have perished in a contest with Apollo."

"They don't seem to have had no luck, any of them," was Leander's depressed conclusion.

"Aphrodite, or Venus, as you choose to call her, took a prominent part in the Trojan war, the origin of which ten years' struggle may be traced to a certain golden apple."

"What an old rag-bag it is!" thought Leander. "I'm only wasting money on him. He's like a bran-pie at a fancy fair : what you get out of him is always the thing you didn't want."

"No, no, Mr. Freemoult," he said, with some impatience; "leave out about the war and the apple. It— it isn't either of them as I wanted to hear about."

"Then I have done," said the old man, curtly. "You've had considerably more than half a crown's worth, as it is."

"Look here, Mr. Freemoult," said the reckless hairdresser, "if you can't give me no better value, I don't mind laying out another sixpence in questions."

"Put your questions, then, by all means; and I'll give you your fair sixpenn'orth of answers. Now, then, I'm ready for you. What's your difficulty? Out with it."

"Why," said Leander, in no small confusion, "isn't there a story somewhere of a statue to Venus as some young man (a long time back it was, of course) was said to have put his ring on? and do you know the rights of it? I—I can't remember how it ended, myself."

"Wait a bit, sir; I think I do remember something of the legend you refer to. You found it in the *Earthly Paradise*, I make no doubt?"

"I found it in Rosherwich Gardens," Leander very nearly blurted out; but he stopped himself, and said instead, "I don't think I've ever been there, sir; not to remember it."

"Well, well! you're no lover of poetry, that's very evident; but the story is there. Yes, yes; and Burton has a version of it, too, in his *Anatomy*. How does it go? Give my head a minute to clear, and I'll tell you. Ha! I have it! It was something like this: There was a certain young gentleman of Rome who, on his wedding-day, went out to play tennis; and in the tennis-court was a brass statue of the goddess Venus——"

("Mine *ought* to be brass, from her goings on," thought Leander.)

"And while he played he took off his finger-ring and put it upon the statue's hand; a mighty foolish act, as you will agree."

"Ah!" said Leander, shaking his head; "you may say that! What next, sir?" He became excited to find that he really was on the right track at last.

"Why, when the game was over, and he came to get his ring, he found he couldn't get it off again. Ha! ha!" and the old man chuckled softly, and then relapsed once more into silence.

"Yes, yes, Mr. Freemoult, sir! I'm a-listening; it's very funny; only do go on!"

"Go on? Where was I? Hadn't I finished? Ah, to be sure! Well, so Paris gave *her* the apple, you see."

"I didn't understand you to allude to no apple," said

his puzzled hearer; "and it was at Rome, I thought, not Paris. Bring your mind more to it, sir; we'd got to the ring not coming off the statue."

"I know, sir; I know. My mind's clear enough, let me tell you. That very night (as I was about to say, if you'd had patience to hear me) Venus stepped in and parted the unfortunate pair——"

"It was a apple just now, you aggravating old muddle 'ed!" said Leander, internally.

"Venus informed the young man that he had betrothed himself to her by that ring" ("Same game exactly," thought the pupil), "and—and, in short, she led him such a life for some nights, that he could bear it no longer. So at length he repaired to a certain mighty magician called—— Let me see, what was his name again? It wasn't Agrippa—was it Albertus? Odd; it has escaped me for the moment."

"Never mind, sir; call him Jones."

"I will *not* call him Jones, sir! I had it on my tongue—there, *Palumbus!* Palumbus it was. Well, Palumbus told him the goddess would never cease to trouble him, unless he could get back the ring—unless he could get back the ring."

Leander's heart began to beat high; the solution of his difficulty was at hand. It was something to know for certain that upon recovery of the ring the goddess's power would be at an end. It only remained to find out how the other young man managed it. "Yes, Mr. Freemoult?" he said interrogatively; for the old gentleman had run down again.

"I was only thinking it out. To resume, then. No sooner had the magician (whose name as I said was Apollonius) come to the wedding, than he promptly conjectured the bride to be a serpent; whereupon she vanished incontinently, after the manner of serpents, with the house and furniture."

"Haven't you missed out a lot, sir?" inquired Leander, deferentially; "because it don't seem to me to hook on quite. What became of Venus and the ring?"

"How the dickens am I to tell you, if you will interrupt? Ring! *What* ring? Why, yes; the magician gave the young man a certain letter, and told him to go to a particular cross-road outside the city, at dead of night, and wait for Saturn to pass by in procession, with his fallen associates. This he did, and presented the magician's letter; which Saturn, after having read, called Venus to him, who was riding in front, and commanded her to deliver up the ring."

Here he stopped, as if he had nothing to add.

"And did she, sir?" asked Leander, breathlessly.

"Did she what? give up the ring? Of course she did. Haven't I been saying so? Why not?"

"Well," observed Leander, "so that's how *he* got out of it, was it? Hah! he was a lucky chap. Those were the days when magicians did a good trade, I suppose? Should you say there were any such parties now, on the quiet like, eh, sir?"

"Bah! Magic is a lost art, degraded to dark séances and juvenile parties—the last magician dead for more than two hundred years. Don't expose your ignorance, sir, by any more such questions."

"No," said Leander; "I thought as much. And so, if any one was to get into such a fix nowadays—of course, that's only my talk, but if they did—there ain't a practising magician anywhere to help him out of it. That's your opinion, ain't it, sir?"

"As the danger of such a contingency is not immediate," was the reply, "the want of a remedy need not, in my humble opinion, cause you any grave uneasiness."

"No," agreed Leander, dejectedly. "I don't care, of course. I was only thinking that, in case—but there, it's no odds! Well, Mr. Freemoult, you've told me what I was curious to know, and here's your little honnyrarium, sir—two shillings and two sixpences, making three shillings in all, pre-cisely."

"Keep your money, sir," said the old man, with contemptuous good humour. "My working hours are done for the day, and you're welcome enough to any instruction you're capable of receiving from my remarks. It's not saying much, I dare say."

"Oh, you told it very clear, considering, sir, I'm sure! I don't grudge it."

"Keep it, I tell you, and say no more about it."

So, expressing his thanks, Leander left the place; and, when he was outside, felt more keenly than ever the blow his hopes had sustained.

He knew the whole story of his predecessor in misfortune now, and, as a precedent, it was worse than useless.

True, for an instant a wild idea had crossed his mind, of seeking some lonely suburban cross-road at dead of night, just to see if anything came of it. "The last time was several hundred years ago, it seems," he told himself; "but there's no saying that Satan mightn't come by, for all that. Here's Venus persecuting as lively as ever, and I never heard the devil was dead. I've a good mind to take the tram to the Archway, and walk out till I find a likely-looking place."

But, on reflection, he gave this up. "If he did come by, I couldn't bring him a line—not even from the conjuror in High 'Oborn—and Satan might make me put my hand to something binding, and I shouldn't be no better off. No; I don't see no way of getting back my ring and poor Tillie's cloak, nor yet getting rid of that goddess, any more than before. There's one comfort, I can't be any worse off than I am."

Oppressed by these gloomy reflections, he returned to his home, expecting a renewal of his nightly persecution from the goddess; but from some cause, into which he was too grateful to care to inquire, the statue that evening showed no sign of life in his presence, and after waiting with the cupboard open for some time in suspense, he ventured to make himself some coffee.

He had scarcely tasted it, however, before he heard, from the passage below, a low whistle, followed by the peculiar stavé by which a modern low-life Blondel endeavours to attract attention. The hairdresser paid no attention, being used, as a Londoner, to hearing such signals, and not imagining they could be intended for his ear.

But presently a handful of gravel rattled against his window, and the whistle was repeated. He went to the window cautiously, and looked out. Below were two individuals, rather carefully muffled; their faces, which were only indistinctly seen, were upturned to him.

He retreated, trembling. He had had so much to think of lately, that the legal danger he was running, by harbouring the detested statue, was almost forgotten; but now he remembered the Inspector's words, and his legs bent beneath him. Could these people be *detectives?*

"Is that Mr. Tweddle up there?" said a voice below —"because if it is, he'd better come down, double quick, and let us in, that's all!"

"'Ere, don't you skulk up there!" added a coarser

" FOR 'ARF A PINT I'D KNOCK YOUR BLOOMIN' 'ED IN ! "

[*Page* 141.

voice. "We know y'er there; and if yer don't come down to us, why, we'll come up to you!"

This brought Leander forward again. "Gentlemen," he said, leaning out, and speaking in an agitated whisper, "for goodness' sake, what do you want with me?"

"You let us in, and we'll tell you."

"Will it do if I come down and speak to you outside?" said Leander.

There was a consultation between the two at this, and at the end of it the first man said: "It's all the same to us, where we have our little confabulation. Come down, and look sharp about it!"

Leander came down, taking care to shut the street door behind him. "You ain't the police?" he said, apprehensively.

They each took an arm, and walked him roughly off between them towards Queen Square. "We'll show you who we are," they said.

"I—I demand your authority for this," gasped Leander. "What am I charged with?"

They had brought him into the gloomiest part of the square, where the houses, used as offices in the daytime, were now dark and deserted. Here they jammed him up against the railings, and stood guard over him, while he was alarmed to perceive a suppressed ferocity in the faces of both.

"What are you charged with? Grr——! For 'arf a pint I'd knock your bloomin 'ed in!" said the coarser gentleman of the two—an evasive form of answer which did not seem to promise a pleasant interview.

Leander was not naturally courageous, and what he had gone through lately had shaken his nerves. He thought that, for policemen, they showed too strong a personal feeling; but who else could they be? He could not remember having seen either of them before. One was a tall, burly, heavy-jawed man; the other smaller and slighter, and apparently the superior of the two in education and position.

"You don't remember me, I see," said the latter; and then suddenly changing his tone to a foreign accent, he said: "Haf you been since to drink a glass of beer at your open-air gardens at Rosherwich?"

Leander knew him then. It was his foreign customer of Monday evening. His face was clean-shaven now, and his expression changed—not for the better.

"I think," he said, faintly, "I had the privilege of cutting your 'air the other evening."

"You did, my friend, and I admired your taste for the fine arts. This gentleman and I have, on talking it over, been so struck by what I saw that evening, that we ventured to call and inquire into it."

"Look 'ere, Count," said his companion, "there ain't time for all that perliteness. You leave him to me; *I'll* talk to him! Now then, you white-livered little airy-sneak, do you know who we are?"

"No," said Leander; "and, excuse me calling of your attention to it, but you're pinching my arm!"

"I'll pinch it off before I've done," said the burly man. "Well, we're the men that have planned and strived, and run all the risk, that you and your gang might cut in and carry off our honest earnings. You infernal little hair-cutting shrimp, you! To think of being beaten by the likes of you! It's sickening, that's what it is, sickening!"

"I don't understand you—as I live, gentlemen, I don't understand you!" pleaded Leander.

"You understand us well enough," said the ex-foreigner, with an awful imprecation on all Leander's salient features; "but you shall have it all in black and white. We're the party that invented and carried out that little job at Wricklesmarsh Court."

"Burglars! Do you mean you're burglars?" cried the terrified Leander.

"We started as burglars, but we've finished by being made cat's-paws of—by you, curse you! You didn't think we should find you out, did you? But if you wanted to keep us in the dark, you made two awkward little slips: one was leaving your name and address at the gardens as the party who was supposed to have last seen the statue, and the other was keeping the said statue standing about in your hair-cutting room, to meet the eye of any gentleman calling out of curiosity, and never expecting such a find as that."

"What's the good of jawing at him, Count? That won't satisfy me, it won't. 'Ere, I can't 'old myself off him any longer. I *must* put a 'ed on him."

But the other interposed. "Patience, my good Braddle. No violence. Leave him to me; he's a devilish deep fellow, and deserves all respect." (Here he shook Leander like a rat.) "You've stolen a march on us, you condemned little hair-dressing ape, you! How did you do it? Out with it! How the devil did you do it?"

"For the love of heaven, gents," pleaded Leander, without reflecting that he might have found a stronger inducement, "don't use violence! How did I do *what?*"

"Count, I *can't* answer for myself," said the man addressed as Braddle. "I shall send a bullet into him if you don't let me work it off with fists; I know I shall!"

"Keep quiet," said his superior, sternly. "Don't you see *I'm* quiet?" and he twisted his knuckles viciously into Leander's throat. "If you call out you're a corpse!"

" I wasn't thinking of calling out, indeed I wasn't. I'm quite satisfied with being where I am," said Leander, " if you'd only leave me a little more room to choke in, and tell me what I've done to put you both in such tremenjous tempers."

" Done ? You cur, when yer know well enough you've taken the bread out of our mouths—the bread we'd earned ! D'ye suppose we left out that statue in the gardens for the like of you? Who put you up to it? How many were there in it ? What do you mean to do now you've got it ? Speak out, or I swear I'll cut your heart out, and throw it over the railings for the tom-cats ; I will, you —— ! "

The man called Braddle, as he uttered this threat, looked so very anxious to execute it, that Leander gave himself up for lost.

" As true as I stand here, gentlemen, I didn't steal that statue."

" I doubt you're not the build for taking the lead in that sort of thing," said the Count ; " but you were in it. You went down that Saturday as a blind. Deny it if you dare."

Leander did not dare. " I could not help myself, gentlemen," he faltered.

" Who said you could ? And you can't help yourself now, either ; so make a clean breast of it. Who are you standing in with? Is it Potter's lot ? "

If Leander had declared himself to be alone, things might have gone harder with him, and they certainly would never have believed him; so he said it *was* Potter's lot.

" I told you Potter was after that marble, and you wouldn't have it, Count," growled Braddle. " Now you're satisfied."

The Count comprised Potter and his lot in a new and original malediction by way of answer, and then said to Leander, " Did Potter tell you to let that Venus stand where all the world might see it?"

" I had no discretion," said the hairdresser. " I'm not responsible, indeed, gents."

" No discretion! I should think you hadn't. Nor Potter either, acting the dog in the manger like this. Where'll *he* find his market for it, eh? What orders have you got? When are you going to get it across?"

" I've no notions. I haven't received no directions," said Leander.

" A nice sort o' mug you are to be trusted with a job like this," said Braddle. " I did think Potter was better up in his work, I did. A pretty bungle he'll make of it!"

" It would serve him right, for interfering with fellow-professionals in this infernal unprincipled manner. But he shan't have the chance, Braddle, he shan't have the chance ; we'll steal a march on him this time."

" Is the coast clear yet?" said Braddle.

" We must risk it. We shall find a route for it, never fear," was the reply. " Now, you cursed hairdresser, you listen to what I'm going to tell you. That Venus is our lawful property, and, by ——, we mean to get her into our hands again. D'ye hear that?"

Leander heard, and with delight. So long as he could once get free from the presence of the statue, and out of the cross-fire of burglars and police, he was willing by this time to abandon the cloak and ring.

" I can truly say, I hope you'll be successful, gents," he replied.

" We don't want your hopes, we want your help. You must round on Potter."

" Must I, gents?" said Leander. "Well, to oblige you, whatever it costs me, I *will* round on Potter."

"Take care you stick to that," said Braddle. "The next pint, Count, is 'ow we're to get her."

"Come in and take her away now," said Leander, eagerly. "She'll be quiet. I—I mean the *house*'ll be quiet. You'll be very welcome, I assure you. *I* won't interfere."

" You're a bright chap to go in for a purfession like ours," said Mr. Braddle, with intense disgust. "How do yer suppose we're to do it—take her to pieces, eh, and bring her along in our pockets? Do you think we're flats enough to run the chance of being seen in the streets by a copper, lugging that 'ere statue along?"

"We must have the light cart again, and a sack," said the Count. "It's too late to-night."

"And it ain't safe in the daytime," said Braddle. "We're wanted for that job at Camberwell, that puts it on to-morrow evening. But suppose Potter has fixed the same time."

"Here, *you* know. Has Potter fixed the same time?" the Count demanded from Leander.

"No," said Leander; "Potter ain't said nothing to me about moving her."

"Then are you man enough to undertake Potter, if he starts the idea? *Are* you? Come!"

"Yes, gents, I'll manage Potter. You break in any time after midnight, and I engage you shall find the Venus on the premises."

" But we want more than that of you, you know. We mustn't lose any time over this job. You must be ready at the door to let us in, and bear a hand with her down to the cart."

But this did not suit Leander's views at all. He was

determined to avoid all personal risks; and to be caught helping the burglars to carry off the Aphrodite would be fatal.

He was recovering his presence of mind. As his tormentors had sensibly relaxed, he was able to take steps for his own security.

"I beg pardon, gents," he said, "but I don't want to appear in this myself. There's Potter, you see; he's a hawful man to go against. You know what Potter is, yourselves." (Potter was really coming in quite usefully, he began to think.)

"Well, I don't suppose Potter would make more bones about slitting your throat than we should, if he knew you'd played him false," said the Count. "But we can't help that; in a place like this it's too risky to break in, when we can be let in."

"If you'll only excuse me taking an active part," said Leander, "it's all I ask. This is my plan, gentlemen. You see that little archway there, where my finger points? Well, that leads by a small alley to a yard, back of my saloon. You can leave your cart here, and come round as safe as you please. I'll have the winder in my saloon unfastened, and put the statue where you can get her easy; but I don't want to be mixed up in it further than that."

"That seems fair enough," said the Count, "provided you keep to it."

"But suppose it's a plant?" growled Braddle. "Suppose he's planning to lay a trap for us? Suppose we get in, to find Potter and his lot on the look-out for us, or break into a house that's full of bloomin' coppers?"

"I did think of that; but I believe our friend knows that if he doesn't act square with me, his life isn't worth a bent pin; and besides, he can't warn the police without getting himself into more or less hot water. So I think he'll see the wisdom of doing what he's told."

"I do," said Leander, "I do, gentlemen. I'd sooner die than deceive you."

"Well," said the Count, "you'd find it come to the same thing."

"No," added Braddle. "If you blow the gaff on us, my bloomin,' I'll saw that pudden head of yours right off your shoulders, and swing for it, cheerful!"

Leander shuddered. Amongst what desperate ruffians had his unlucky stars led him! How would it all end, he wondered feebly—how?

"Well, gentlemen," he said, with his teeth chattering, "if you don't want me any more, I'll go in; and I'm to expect you to-morrow evening, I believe?"

"Expect us when you 'ear us," said Braddle; "and if you make fools of us again——" And he described consequences which exceeded in unpleasantness the worst that Leander could have imagined.

The poor man tottered back to his room again, in a most unenviable frame of mind; not even the prospect of being delivered from the goddess could reconcile him to the price he must pay for it. He was going to take a plunge into downright crime now; and if his friend the inspector came to hear of it, ruin must follow. And, in any case, the cloak and the ring would be gone beyond recovery, while these cut-throat housebreakers would henceforth have a hold over him; they might insist upon steeping him in blacker crime still, and he knew he would never have the courage to resist.

As he thought of the new difficulties and dangers that compassed him round about, he was frequently on the verge of tears, and his couch that night was visited by dreadful dreams, in which he sought audience of the Evil One himself at cross-roads, was chased over half London by police, and dragged over the other half by burglars, to be finally flattened by the fall of Aphrodite.

AT LAST

IX

> " Does not the stone rebuke me
> For being more stone than it?"
>
> *Winter's Tale.*

> "Yet did he loath to see the image fair,
> White and unchanged of face, unmoved of limb!"
>
> *Earthly Paradise.*

LEANDER'S hand was very tremulous all the next day, as several indignant clients discovered, and he closed as early as he could, feeling it impossible to attend to business under the circumstances.

About seven o'clock he went up to his sitting-room. A difficult and ungrateful task was before him. To facilitate her removal, he must persuade the goddess to take up a position in the saloon for the night; and, much as he had suffered from her, there was something traitorous in delivering her over to these coarse burglars.

He waited until the statue showed signs of returning animation, and then said, "Good evening, mum," more obsequiously than usual.

She never deigned to notice or return his salutations. "Hairdresser," she said abruptly, "I am weary of this sordid place."

He was pleased, for it furthered his views. "It isn't

153

so sordid in the saloon, where you stood the other evening, you know," he replied. " Will you step down there ? "

" Bah ! " she said, " it is *all* sordid.   Leander, a restlessness has come upon me.   I come back night after night out of the vagueness in which I have lain so long, and for what ?   To stand here in this mean chamber and proffer my favour, only to find it repulsed, disdained. I am tired of it—tired ! "

" You can't be more tired of it than I am ! " he said.

" I ask myself," she went on, " why, having, through your means, ascended once more to the earth, which I left so fair, I seek not those things which once delighted me.   This city of yours—all that I have seen of it— revolts me ; but it is vast, vaster than those built by the mortals of old.   Surely somewhere there must be brightness in it and beauty, and the colour and harmony by which men knew once to delight the gods themselves.   It cannot be that the gods of old are all forgotten ; surely, somewhere there yet lingers a little band of faithful ones, who have not turned from Aphrodite."

" I can't say, I'm sure," said Leander ; " I could inquire for you."

" I myself will seek for them," she said proudly.   " I will go forth this very night."

Leander choked.   " To-night ! " he cried.   " You *can't* go to-night."

" You forget yourself," she returned haughtily.

" If I let you go," he said hesitatingly, " will you promise faithfully to be back in half an hour ? "

" Do you not yet understand that you have to do with a goddess—with Aphrodite herself ? " she said. " Who are you, to presume to fetter me by your restrictions ?   Truly, the indulgence I have shown has turned your weak brain."

He put his back against the door. He was afraid of the goddess, but he was still more afraid of the burglars' vengeance if they arrived to find the prize missing.

"I'm sorry to disoblige a lady," he said ; "but you don't go out of this house to-night."

In another minute he was lying in the fender amongst the fireirons—alone ! How it was done he was too stunned to remember ; but the goddess was gone. If she did not return by midnight, what would become of him ? If he had only been civil to her, she might have stayed ; but now she had abandoned him to certain destruction !

A kind of fatalistic stupor seized him. He would not run away—he would have to come home some time —nor would he call in the police, for he had a very vivid recollection of Mr. Braddle's threat in such a contingency.

He went, instead, into the dark saloon, and sat down in a chair to wait. He wondered how he could explain the statue's absence. If he told the burglars it had gone for a stroll, they would tear him limb from limb. "I was so confoundedly artful about Potter," he thought bitterly, "that they'll never believe now I haven't warned him ! "

At every sound outside he shook like a leaf ; the quarters, as they sounded from the church clock, sank like cold weights upon his heart. "If only Venus would come back first !" he moaned ; but the statue never returned.

At last he heard steps—muffled ones—on the paved alley outside. He had forgotten to leave the window unfastened, after all, and he was too paralysed to do it now.

The steps were in the little yard, or rather a sort of back area, underneath the window. "It may be only a constable," he tried to say to himself; but there is no mistaking the constabulary tread, which is not fairy-like, or even gentle, like that he heard.

A low whistle destroyed his last hope. In a quite unpremeditated manner he put out the gas and rolled under a leather divan which stood at the end of the room. He wished now, with all his heart, that he had run away while he had the chance ; but it was too late.

"I hope they'll do it with a revolver, and not a knife," he thought. "Oh, my poor Matilda ! you little know what I'm going through just now, and what'll be going through *me* in another minute !"

A hoarse voice under the window called out, "Tweddle !"

He lay still. "None o' that, yer skulker; I know yer there !" said the voice again. "Do yer want to give me the job o' coming after yer ?"

After all, Leander reflected, there was the window and a thick half-shutter between them. It might be best not to provoke Mr. Braddle at the outset. He came half out of his hiding-place. "Is that you, Mr. Braddle ?" he quavered.

"Ah !" said the voice, affirmatively. "Is this what you call being ready for us? Why, the bloomin' winder ain't even undone !"

"That's what I'm here for," said poor Leander. "Is the—the other gentleman out there too ?"

"You mind your business ! You'll find something the Count give me to bring yer; I've put it on the winder-sill out 'ere. And you obey horders next time, will yer ?"

The footsteps were heard retreating. Mr. Braddle was apparently going back to fetch his captain. Leander let down the shutter, and opened the window. He could not see, but he could feel a thick, rough bundle lying on the window-sill.

He drew this in, slammed down the window, and ran up the shutter in a second, before the two could have had time to discover him.

" Now," he thought, " I *will* run for it ; " and he groped his way out of the dark saloon to the front shop, where he paused, and, taking a match from his pocket, struck a light. His parcel proved to be rough sackcloth, on the outside of which a paper was pinned.

Why did the Count write, when he was coming in directly ? Curiosity made him linger even then to ascertain this. The paper contained a hasty scrawl in blue chalk. " *Not to-night,*" he read ; " *arrangements still uncomplete. Expect us to-morrow night without fail, and see that everything is prepared. Cloth sent with this for packing goods. P—— laid up with professional accident, and safe for a week or two. You must have known this—why not say so last night ? No trifling, if you value life !*"

It was a reprieve—at the last moment ! He had a whole day before him for flight, and he fully intended to flee this time ; those hours of suspense in the saloon were too terrible to be gone through twice.

But as he was turning out his cashbox, and about to go upstairs and collect a few necessaries, he heard a well-known tread outside. He ran to the door, which he unfastened with trembling hands, and the statue, with the hood drawn closely round her strange painted face, passed in without seeming to heed his presence.

She had come back to him. Why should he run away now, when, if he waited one more night, he might be rescued from one of his terrors by means of the other ?

"Lady Venus!" he cried hysterically. "Oh, Lady Venus, mum, I thought you was gone for ever!"

"And you have grieved?" she said almost tenderly. "You welcome my return with joy! Know then, Leander, that I myself feel pleasure in returning, even to such a roof as this; for little gladness have I had from my wanderings. Upon no altar did I see my name shine, nor the perfumed flame flicker; the Lydian measures were silent, and the praise of Cytherea. And everywhere I went I found the same senseless troubled haste, and pale mean faces of men, and squalor, and tumult. Grace and joyousness have fled—even from your revelry! But I have seen your new gods, and understand: for, all grimy and mis-shapen and uncouth are they as they stand in your open places and at the corners of your streets. Zeus, what a place must Olympus now be! And can any men worship such monsters, and be gladsome?"

Leander did not perceive the very natural mistake into which the goddess had fallen; but the fact was, that she had come upon some of our justly renowned public statues.

"I'm sorry you haven't enjoyed yourself, mum," was all he could find to say.

"Should I linger in such scenes were it not for you?" she cried reproachfully. "How much longer will you repulse me?"

"That depends on you, mum," he ventured to observe.

"Ah! you are cold!" she said reproachfully; "yet surely I am worthy of the adoration of the proudest mortal. Judge me not by this marble exterior, cunningly wrought though it be. Charms are mine, more dazzling than any your imagination can picture; and could you surrender your being to my hands, I should be able to show myself as I really am—supreme in loveliness and majesty!"

Unfortunately, the hairdresser's imagination was not his strongest point. He could not dissociate the goddess from the marble shape she had assumed, and that shape he was not sufficiently educated to admire; he merely coughed now in a deferential manner.

" I perceive that I cannot move you," she said. " Men have grown strangely stubborn and impervious. I leave you, then, to your obstinacy; only take heed lest you provoke me at last to wrath, for my patience is well-nigh at an end!"

And she was gone, and the bedizened statue stood there, staring hardly at him with the eyes his own hand had given her.

"This has been the most trying evening I've had yet," he thought. "Thank my stars, if all goes well, I shall get rid of her by this time to-morrow!"

The next day passed uneventfully enough, though the unfortunate Leander's apprehensions increased with every hour. As before, he closed early, got his apprentice safely off the premises, and sat down to wait in his saloon. He knew that the statue (which he had concealed during the day behind a convenient curtain) would probably recover consciousness for some part of the evening, as it had rarely failed to do, and prudence urged him to keep an eye over the proceedings of his tormentress.

To his horror, Aphrodite's first words, after awaking, expressed her intention of repeating the search for homage and beauty, which had been so unsuccessful the night before!

"Seek not to detain me, Leander," she said; " for, goddess as I am, I am drooping under this persistent obduracy. Somewhere beyond this murky labyrinth, it may be that I shall find a shrine where I am yet honoured. I will go forth, and never rest till I have found it, and my troubled spirits are revived by the incense for which I have languished so long. I am weary of abasing myself to such a contemptuous mortal, nor will I longer endure such indignity. Stand back, and open the gates for me! Why do you not obey?"

He knew now that to attempt force would be useless; and yet if she left him this time, he must either abandon all that life held for him, and fly to distant parts from the burglars' vengeance—or remain to meet a too probable doom!

He fell on his knees before her. "Oh, Lady Venus," he entreated, "don't leave me! I beg and implore you not to! If you do, you will kill me! I give you my honest word you will!"

The statue's face seemed irradiated by a sudden joy. She paused, and glanced down with an approving smile upon the kneeling figure at her feet.

"Why did you not kneel to me before?" she said.

"Because I never thought of it," said the hairdresser, honestly; "but I'll stay on my knees for hours, if only you won't go!"

"But what has made you thus eager, thus humble?" she said, half in wonder and half in suspicion. "Can it be, that the spark I have sought to kindle in your breast is growing to a flame at last? Leander, can this thing be?"

He saw that she was gratified, that she desired to be assured that this was indeed so.

"I shouldn't be surprised if something like that was going on inside of me," he said encouragingly.

"Answer me more frankly," she said. "Do you wish

SHAVING 2
HAIR CUTTING 6
SINGEING . . 4
SHAMPOOING 6

"WHY DID YOU NOT KNEEL TO ME BEFORE?"

[Page 160.

me to remain with you because you have learnt to love
my presence?"

It was a very embarrassing position for him. All
depended upon his convincing the goddess of his dawning
love, and yet, for the life of him, he could not force out
the requisite tenderness; his imagination was unequal to
the task.

Another and a more creditable feeling helped to tie
his tongue—a sense of shame at employing such a
subterfuge in order to betray the goddess into the
lawless hands of these housebreakers. However, she
must be induced to stay by some means.

"Well," he said sheepishly, "you don't give me a
chance to love you, if you go wandering out every
evening, do you?"

She gave a low cry of triumph. "It has come!"
she exclaimed. "What are clouds of incense, flowers,
and homage, to this? Be of good heart; I will stay,
Leander. Fear not, but speak the passion which
consumes you!"

He became alarmed. He was anxious not to commit
himself, and yet employ the time until the burglars might
be expected.

"The fact is," he confessed, "it hasn't gone so far as
that yet—it's beginning; all it wants is *time*, you know—
time, and being let alone."

"All Time will be before us, when once your lips
have pronounced the words of surrender, and our spirits
are transported together to the enchanted isle."

"You talk about me going over to this isle—this
Cyprus," he said; "but it's a long journey, and I can't
afford it. How *you* come and go, I don't know; but I've
not been brought up to it myself. I can't flash across
like a telegram!"

"Trust all to me," she said. "Is not your love strong enough for that?"

"Not quite yet," he answered; "it's coming on. Only, you see, it's a serious step to take, and I naturally wish to feel my way. I declare, the more I gaze upon the—the elegant form and figger which I see before me, the stronger and the more irresistible comes over me a burning desire to think the whole thing carefully over. And if you only allowed me a little longer to gaze (I've no time to myself except in the evenings), I don't think it would be long before this affair reached a 'appy termination—I don't indeed!"

"Gaze, then," she said, smiling—"gaze to your soul's content."

"I mean no offence," he represented, having felt his way to a stroke of supreme cunning, "but when I feel there's a goddess inside of this statue, I don't know how it is exactly, but it puts me off. I can't fix my thoughts; the—the passion don't ferment as it ought. If, supposing now, you was to withdraw yourself and leave me the statue? I could gaze on it, and think of thee, and Cyprus, and all the rest of it, more comfortable, so to speak, than what I can when you're animating of it, and making me that nervous, words can't describe it!"

He hardly dared to hope that so lame and transparent a device would succeed with her; but, as he had previously found, there was a certain spice of credulity and simplicity in her nature, which made it possible to impose upon her occasionally.

"It may be so," she said. "I overawe thee, perchance?"

"Very much so," said he, promptly. "You don't intend it, I know; but it's a fact."

"I will leave you to meditate upon the charms so

faintly shadowed in this image, remembering that whatever of loveliness you find herein will be multiplied ten
thousand-fold in the actual Aphrodite ! Remain, then ;
ponder and gaze—and love ! "

He waited for a little while after the statue was silent,
and then took up the sacking left for him by Braddle ;
twice he attempted to throw it over the marble, and
twice he recoiled. " It's no use," he said, " I can't do it ;
they must do it themselves ! "

He carefully unfastened the window at the back of
his saloon, and, placing the statue in the centre of the
floor, turned out the gas, and with a beating heart stole
upstairs to his bedroom, where (with his door bolted)
he waited anxiously for the arrival of his dreaded
deliverers.

He scarcely knew how long he had been there, for a
kind of waking dream had come upon him, in which he
was providing the statue with light refreshment in the
shape of fancy pebbles and liquid cement, when the long,
low whistle, faintly heard from the back of the house,
brought him back to his full senses.

The burglars had come ! He unbolted the door and
stole out to the top of the crazy staircase, intending to
rush back and bolt himself in if he heard steps ascending ;
and for some minutes he strained his ears, without being
able to catch a sound.

At last he heard the muffled creak of the window, as
it was thrown up. They were coming in ! Would they,
or would they not, be inhuman enough to force him to
assist them in the removal ?

They were still in the saloon ; he heard them tramp-
ling about, moving the furniture with unnecessary
violence, and addressing one another in tones that were
not caressing. Now they were carrying the statue to the

window ; he heard their labouring breath and groans of exertion under the burden.

Another pause. He stole lower down the staircase, until he was outside his sitting-room, and could hear better. There ! that was the thud as they leapt out on the flagged yard. A second and heavier thud—the goddess ! How would they get her over the wall ? Had they brought steps, ropes, or what ? No matter ; they knew their own business, and were not likely to have forgotten anything. But how long they were about it ! Suppose a constable were to come by and see the cart !

There were sounds at last ; they were scaling the wall—floundering, apparently ; and no wonder, with such a weight to hoist after them ! More thuds ; and then the steps of men staggering slowly, painfully away. The steps echoed louder from under the archway, and then died away in silence.

Could they be really gone ? He dared not hope so, and remained shivering in his sitting-room for some minutes ; until, gaining courage, he determined to go down and shut the window, to avoid any suspicion. Although now that the burglars were safely off with their prize, even their capture could not implicate him. He rather hoped they *would* be caught !

He took a lighted candle, and descended. As he entered the saloon, a gust from the open window blew out the light. He stood there in the dark and an icy draught ; and, beginning to grope about in the dark for the matches, he brushed against something which was soft and had a cloth-like texture. " It's Braddle ! " he thought, and his blood ran cold ; " or else the Count ! " And he called them both respectfully. There was no reply ; no sound of breathing, even.

Ha ! here was a box of matches at last ! He struck

a light in feverish haste, and lit the nearest gas-bracket.
For an instant he could see nothing, in the sudden glare;
but the next moment he fell back against the wall with a
cry of horror and despair.

For there, in the centre of the disordered room, stood
—not the Count, not Braddle—but the statue, the
mantle thrown back from her arms, and those arms, and
the folds of the marble drapery, spotted here and there
with stains of dark crimson !

DAMOCLES DINES OUT

X.

"To feed were best at home."—*Macbeth.*

As soon as Leander had recovered from the first shock
of horror and disappointment, he set himself to efface
the stains with which the statue and the oilcloth were
liberally bespattered; he was burning to find out what
had happened to make such desperadoes abandon their
design at the point of completion.

They both seemed to have bled freely. Had they
quarrelled, or what? He went out into the yard with
a hand-lamp, trembling lest he should come upon one or
more corpses; but the place was bare, and he then
remembered having heard them stumble and flounder
over the wall.

He came back in utter bewilderment; the statue,
standing calm and lifeless as he had himself placed it,
could tell him nothing, and he went back to his bedroom
full of the vaguest fears.

The next day was a Saturday, and he passed it in the
state of continual apprehension which was becoming his
normal condition. He expected every moment to see or
hear from the baffled ruffians, who would, no doubt, consider him responsible for their failure; but no word nor
sign came from them, and the uncertainty drove him
very near distraction.

As the night approached, he almost welcomed it, as a time when the goddess herself would enlighten part of his ignorance; and he waited more impatiently than ever for her return.

He was made to wait long that evening, until he almost began to think that the marble was deserted altogether; but at length, as he watched, the statue gave a long, shuddering sigh, and seemed to gaze round the saloon with vacant eyes.

" Where am I ? " she murmured. " Ah ! I remember. Leander, while you slumbered, impious hands were laid upon this image ! "

" Dear me, mum; you don't say so ! " exclaimed Leander.

" It is the truth ! From afar I felt the indignity that was purposed, and hastened to protect my image, to find it in the coarse grasp of godless outlaws. Leander, they were about to drag me away by force—away from thee ! "

" I'm very sorry you should have been disturbed," said Leander; and he certainly was. " So you came back and caught them at it, did you ? And wh—what did you do to 'em, if I may inquire ? "

" I know not," she said simply. " I caused them to be filled with mad fury, and they fell upon one another blindly, and fought like wild beasts around my image until strength failed them, and they sank to the ground; and when they were able, they fled from my presence, and I saw them no more."

" You—you didn't kill them outright, then ? " said Leander, not feeling quite sure whether he would be glad or not to hear that they had forfeited their lives.

" They were unworthy of such a death," she said; " so I let them crawl away. Henceforth they will respect our images."

"I should say they would, most likely, madam," agreed Leander. "I do assure you, I'm almost glad of it myself—I am; it served them both right."

"*Almost* glad! And do you not rejoice from your heart that I yet remain to you?"

"Why," said Leander, "it is, in course, a most satisfactory and agreeable termination, I'm sure."

"Who knows whether, if this my image had once been removed from you, I could have found it in my power to return?" she said; "for, I ween, the power that is left me has limits. I might never have appeared to you again. Think of it, Leander."

"I was thinking of it," he replied. "It quite upsets me to think how near it was."

"You are moved. You love me well, do you not, Leander?"

"Oh! I suppose I do," he said—"well enough."

"Well enough to abandon this gross existence, and fly with me where none can separate us?"

"I never said nothing about that," he answered.

"But yesternight and you confessed that you were yielding—that ere long I should prevail."

"So I am," he said; "but it will take me some time to yield thoroughly. You wouldn't believe how slow I yield; why, I haven't hardly begun yet!"

"And how long a time will pass before you are fully prepared?"

"I'm afraid I can't say, not exactly; it may be a month, or it might only be a week, or again, it may be a year. I'm so dependent upon the weather. So, if you're in any kind of a hurry, I couldn't advise you, as a honest man, to wait for me."

"I will not wait a year!" she said fiercely. "You mock me with such words. I tell you again that my forbearance will last but little longer. More of this laggard love, and I will shame you before your fellow-men as an ingrate and a dastard! I will; by my zone, I will!"

"Now, mum, you're allowing yourself to get excited," said Leander, soothingly. "I wouldn't talk about it no more this evening; we shall do no good. I can't arrange to go with you just yet, and there's an end of it."

"You will find that that is not the end of it, clod-witted slave that you are!"

"Now, don't call names; it's beneath you."

"Ay, indeed! for are not *you* beneath me? But for very shame I will not abandon what is justly mine; nor shall you, wily and persuasive hairdresser though you be, withstand my sovereign will with impunity!"

"So you say, mum!" said Leander, with a touch of his native impertinence.

"As I say, I shall act; but no more of this, or you will anger me before the time. Let me depart."

"I'm not hindering you," he said; but she did not remain long enough to resent his words. He sat down with a groan. "Whatever will become of me?" he soliloquized dismally. "She gets more pressing every evening, and she's been taking to threatening dreadful of late. . . . If the Count and that Braddle ever come back now, it won't be to take her off my hands; it'll more likely be to have my life for letting them into such a trap. They'll think it was some trick of mine, I shouldn't wonder. . . . And to-morrow's Sunday, and I've got to dine with aunt, and meet Matilda and her ma. A pretty state of mind I'm in for going out to dinner, after the awful week I've had of it! But there'll be some comfort in seeing my darling Tillie again; *she* ain't a statue, bless her!"

"As for you, mum," he said to the unconscious statue, "I'm going to lock you up in your old quarters, where you can't get out and do mischief. I do think I'm entitled to have my Sunday quiet."

After which he contrived to toil upstairs with the image, not without considerable labour and frequent halts to recover his breath; for although, as we have already noted, the marble, after being infused with life, seemed to lose something of its normal weight, it was no light burden, even then, to be undertaken single-handed.

He slept long and late that Sunday morning; for he had been too preoccupied for the last few days to make any arrangements for attending chapel with his Matilda, and he was in sore need of repose besides. So he rose just in time to swallow his coffee and array himself carefully for his aunt's early dinner, leaving his two Sunday papers—the theatrical and the general organs—unread on his table.

It was a foggy, dull day, and Millman Street, never a cheerful thoroughfare, looked gloomier than ever as he turned into it. But one of those dingy fronts held Matilda—a circumstance which irradiated the entire district for him.

He had scarcely time to knock before the door was opened by Matilda in person. She looked more charming than ever, in a neat dark dress, with a little white collar and cuffs. Her hair was arranged in a new fashion, being banded by a neat braided tress across the crown; and her grey eyes, usually serene and cold, were bright and eager.

The hairdresser felt his heart swell with love at the sight of her. What a lucky man he was, after all, to have such a girl as this to care for him! If he could keep her —ah, if he could only keep her!

175

"I told your aunt *I* was going to open the door to you," she said. "I wanted—— Oh, Leander, you've not brought it, after all!"

"Meaning what, Tillie, my darling?" said Leander.

"Oh, you know—my cloak!"

He had had so much to think about that he had really forgotten the cloak of late.

"Well, no, I've not brought that—not the cloak, Tillie," he said slowly.

"What a time they are about it!" complained Matilda.

"You see," explained the poor man, "when a cloak like that is damaged, it has to be sent back to the manufacturers to be done, and they've so many things on their hands. I couldn't promise that you'll have that cloak—well, not this side of Christmas, at least."

"You must have been very rough with it, then, Leander," she remarked.

"I was," he said. "I don't know how I came to *be* so rough. You see, it was trying to tear it off——" But here he stopped.

"Trying to tear it off what?"

"Trying to tear it off nothink, but trying to tear the wrapper off *it*. It was so involved," he added, "with string and paper and that; and I'm a clumsy, unlucky sort of chap, sweet one; and I'm uncommon sorry about it, that I am!"

"Well, we won't say any more about it," said Matilda, softened by his contrition. "And I'm keeping you out in the passage all this time. Come in, and be introduced to mamma; she's in the front parlour, waiting to make your acquaintance."

Mrs. Collum was a stout lady, with a thin voice. She struck a nameless fear into Leander's soul as he was led

SHE STRUCK A NAMELESS FEAR INTO LEANDER'S SOUL.

[Page 176.

up to where she sat. · He thought that she contained all
the promise of a very terrible mother-in-law.

"This is Leander, mamma dear," said Matilda, shyly
and yet proudly.

Her mother inspected him for a moment, and then
half closed her eyes. "My daughter tells me that you
carry on the occupation of a hairdresser," she said.

"Quite correct, madam," said Leander; "I do."

"Ah! well," she said, with an unconcealed sigh, "I
could have wished to look higher than hairdressing for
my Matilda; but there are opportunities of doing good
even as a hairdresser. I trust you are sensible of
that."

"I try to do as little 'arm as I can," he said feebly.

"If you do not do good, you must do harm," she
said uncompromisingly. "You have it in your means
to be an awakening influence. No one knows the power
that a single serious hairdresser might effect with worldly
customers. Have you never thought of that?"

"Well, I can't say I have exactly," he said; "and I
don't see how."

"There are cheap and appropriate illuminated texts,"
she said, "to be had at so much a dozen; you could
hang them on your walls. There are tracts you procure
by the hundred; you could put them in the lining of
hats as you hang them up; you could wrap them round
your—your bottles and pomatum-pots. You could drop
a word in season in your customer's ear as you bent over
him. And you tell me you don't see how; you *will* not
see, I fear, Mr. Tweddle."

"I'm afraid, mum," he replied, "my customers would
consider I was taking liberties."

"And what of that, so long as you save them?"

"Well, you see, I shouldn't—I should *lose* 'em! And

it's not done in our profession; and, to tell you the honest truth, I'm not given that way myself—not to the extent of tracks and suchlike, that is."

Matilda's mother groaned; it was hard to find a son-in-law with whom she had nothing in common, and who was a hairdresser into the bargain.

"Well, well," she said, "we must expect crosses in this life; though for my own daughter to lay this one upon me is—is—— But I will not repine."

"I'm sorry you regard me in the light of a cross," said Leander; "but, whether I'm a cross or a naught, I'm a respectable man, and I love your daughter, mum, and I'm in a position to maintain her."

Leander hated to have to appear under false pretences, of which he had had more than enough of late. He was glad now to speak out plainly, particularly as he had no reason to fear this old woman.

"Hush, Leander! Mamma didn't mean to be unkind; "did you, mamma?" said Matilda.

"I said what I felt," she said. "We will not discuss it further. If, in time, I see reason for bestowing my blessing upon a choice which at present—— But no matter. If I see reason in time, I will not withhold it. I can hardly be expected to approve at present."

"You shall take your own time, mum; *I* won't hurry you," said Leander. "Tillie is blessing enough for me—not but what I shall be glad to be on a pleasant footing with you, I'm sure, if you can bring yourself to it."

Before Mrs. Collum could reply, Miss Louisa Tweddle made an opportune appearance, to the relief of Matilda, in whom her mother's attitude was causing some uneasiness.

Miss Tweddle was a well-preserved little woman, with

short curly iron-grey hair and sharp features. In manner she was brisk, not to say chirpy, but she secreted sentiment in large quantities. She was very far from the traditional landlady, and where she lost lodgers occasionally she retained friends. She regarded Mrs. Collum with something like reverence, as an acquaintance of her youth who had always occupied a superior social position, and she was proud, though somewhat guiltily so, that her favourite nephew should have succeeded in captivating the daughter of a dentist.

She kissed Leander on both cheeks. "He's done the best of all my nephews, Mrs. Collum, ma'am," she explained, "and he's never caused me a moment's anxiety since I first had the care of him, when he was first apprenticed to Catchpole's in Holborn, and paid me for his board."

"Well, well," said Mrs. Collum, "I hope he never may cause anxiety to you, or to any one."

"I'll answer for it, he won't," said his aunt. "I wish you could see him dress a head of hair."

Mrs. Collum shut her eyes again. "If at his age he has not acquired the necessary skill for his line in life," she observed, "it would be a very melancholy thing to reflect upon."

"Yes, wouldn't it?" agreed Miss Tweddle; "you say very truly, Mrs. Collum. But he's got ideas and notions beyond what you'd expect in a hairdresser—haven't you, Leandy? Tell Miss Collum's dear ma about the new machines you've invented for altering people's hands and eyes and features."

"I don't care to be told," the lady struck in. "To my mind, it's nothing less than sheer impiety to go improving the features we've been endowed with. We ought to be content as we are, and be thankful we've

been sent into the world with any features at all. Those
are my opinions!"

"Ah," said the politic Leander, "but some people
are saved having resort to Art for improvement, and we
oughtn't to blame them as are less favoured for trying to
render themselves more agreeable as spectacles, ought we?"

"And if every one thought with you," added his aunt,
with distinctly inferior tact, "where would your poor
dear 'usband have been, Mrs. Collum, ma'am?"

"My dear husband was not on the same level—he
was a medical man; and, besides, though he replaced
Nature in one of her departments, he had too much
principle to *imitate* her. Had he been (or had I allowed
him to be) less conscientious, his practice would have
been largely extended; but I can truthfully declare that
not a single one of his false teeth was capable of deceiving
for an instant. I hope," she added to Leander, "you, in
your own different way, are as scrupulous."

"Why, the fact is," said Leander, whose professional
susceptibilities were now aroused, "I am essentially an
artist. When I look around, I see that Nature out of its
bounty has supplied me with a choice selection of patterns
to follow, and I reproduce them as faithful as lies within
my abilities. You may call it a fine thing to take a
blank canvas, and represent the luxurious tresses and the
blooming hue of 'ealth upon it, and so do I; but I call it
a still higher and nobler act to produce a similar effect
upon a human 'ed!"

"Isn't that a pretty speech for a young man like him
—only twenty-seven—Mrs. Collum?" exclaimed his
admiring aunt.

"You see, mamma dear," pleaded Matilda, who saw
that her parent remained unaffected, "it isn't as if Leander
was in poor papa's profession."

" I hope, Matilda," said the lady sharply, "you are
not going to pain me again by mentioning this young
man and your departed father in the same breath,
because I cannot bear it."

"The old lady," reflected Leander here, "don't
seem to take to me !"

" I'm sure," said Miss Tweddle, " Leandy quite feels
what an honour it is to him to look forward to such a
connection as yours is. When I first heard of it, I said
at once, 'Leandy, you can't never mean it; she won't
look at you; it's no use your asking her,' I said. And
I quite scolded myself for ever bringing them together !"

Mrs. Collum seemed inclined to follow suit, but she
restrained herself. "Ah ! well," she observed, " my
daughter has chosen to take her own way, without
consulting my prejudices. All I hope is, that she may
never repent it !"

"Very handsomely said, ma'am," chimed in Miss
Tweddle; "and, if I know my nephew, repent it she
never will !"

Leander was looking rather miserable; but Matilda
put out her hand to him behind his aunt's back, and
their eyes and hands met, and he was happy again.

"You must be wanting your dinner, Mrs. Collum,"
his aunt proceeded; "and we are only waiting for
another lady and gentleman to make up the party. I
don't know what's made them so behindhand, I'm sure.
He's a very pleasant young man, and punctual to the
second when he lodged with me. I happened to run
across him up by Chancery Lane the other evening, and
he said to me, in his funny way, ' I've been and gone
and done it, Miss Tweddle, since I saw you. I'm a
happy man ; and I'm thinking of bringing my young lady
soon to introduce to you.' So I asked them to come

and take a bit of dinner with me to-day, and I told him two o'clock sharp, I'm sure. Ah, there they are at last! That's Mr. Jauncy's knock, among a thousand."

Leander started. "Aunt!" he cried, "you haven't asked Jauncy here to-day?"

"Yes, I did, Leandy. I knew you used to be friends when you were together here, and I thought how nice it would be for both your young ladies to make each other's acquaintance; but I didn't tell *him* anything. I meant it for a surprise."

And she bustled out to receive her guests, leaving Leander speechless. What if the new-comers were to make some incautious reference to that pleasure-party on Saturday week? Could he drop them a warning hint?

"Don't you like this Mr. Jauncy, Leander?" whispered Matilda, who had observed his ghastly expression.

"I like him well enough," he returned, with an effort; "but I'd rather we had no third parties, I must say."

Here Mr. Jauncy came in alone, Miss Tweddle having retired to assist the lady to take off her bonnet.

Leander went to meet him. "James," he said in an agitated whisper, "have you brought Bella?"

Jauncy nodded. "We were talking of you as we came along," he said in the same tone, "and I advise you to look out—she's got her quills up, old chap!"

"What about?" murmured Leander.

Mr. Jauncy's grin was wider and more appreciative than ever as he replied, mysteriously, "Rosherwich!"

Leander would have liked to ask in what respect Miss Parkinson considered herself injured by the expedition to Rosherwich; but, before he could do so, his aunt returned with the young lady in question.

Bell was gorgeously dressed, and made her entrance with the stiffest possible dignity. "Miss Parkinson, my dear," said her hostess, "you mustn't be made a stranger of. That lady sitting there on the sofa is Mrs. Collum, and this gentleman is a friend of *your* gentleman's, and my nephew, Leandy."

"Oh, thank you," said Bella, "but I've no occasion to be told Mr. Tweddle's name; we have met before— haven't we, Mr. Tweddle?"

He looked at her, and saw her brows clouded, and her nose and mouth with a pinched look about them. She was annoyed with him evidently—but why?

"We have," was all he could reply.

"Why, how nice that is, to be sure!" exclaimed his aunt. "I might have thought of it, too, Mr. Jauncy, and you being such friends and all. And p'r'aps you know this lady, too—Miss Collum—as Leandy is keeping company along with?"

Bella's expression changed to something blacker still. "No," she said, fixing her eyes on the still unconscious Leander; "I made sure that Mr. Tweddle was courting *a* young lady, but—but—well, this *is* a surprise, Mr. Tweddle! You never told us of this when last we met. I shall have news for somebody!"

"Oh, but it's only been arranged within the last month or two!" said Miss Tweddle.

"Considering we met so lately, he might have done us the compliment of mentioning it, I must say!" said Bella.

"I—I thought you knew," stammered the hairdresser; "I told——"

"No, you didn't, excuse me; oh no, you didn't, or some things would have happened differently. It was the place and all that made you forget it, very likely."

"When did you meet one another, and where was it, Miss Parkinson?" inquired Matilda, rather to include herself in the conversation than from any devouring curiosity.

Leander struck in hoarsely. "We met," he explained, "some time since, quite casual."

Bella's eyes lit up with triumphant malice. "What!" she said, "do you call yesterday week such a long while? What a compliment that is, though! And so he's not even mentioned it to you, Miss Collum? Dear me, I wonder what reasons he had for that, now!"

"There's nothing to wonder at," said Leander; "my memory does play me tricks of that sort."

"Ah, if it was only you it played tricks on! There's Miss Collum dying to know what it's all about, I can see."

"Indeed, Miss Parkinson, I'm nothing of the sort," retorted Matilda, proudly. Privately her reflection was: "She's got a lovely gown on, but she's a common girl, for all that; and she's trying to set me against Leander for some reason, and she shan't do it."

"Well," said Bella, "you're a fortunate man, Mr. Tweddle, that you are, in every way. I'm afraid I shouldn't be so easy with my James."

"There's no need for being afraid about it," her James put in; "you aren't!"

"I hope you haven't as much cause, though," she retorted.

Leander listened to her malicious innuendo with a bewildered agony. Why on earth was she making this dead set at him? She was amiable enough on Saturday week. It never occurred to him that his conduct to her sister could account for it, for had he not told Ada straightforwardly how he was situated?

Fortunately dinner was announced to be ready just then, and Bella was silenced for the moment in the general movement to the next room.

Leander took in Matilda's mamma, who had been studiously abstracting herself from all surrounding objects for the last few minutes. "That Bella is a downright basilisk," he thought dismally, as he led the way. "Lord, how I do wish dinner was done!"

DENOUNCED

XI.

"There's a new foot on the floor, my friend;
  And a new face at the door, my friend;
  A new face at the door."

LEANDER sat at the head of the table as carver, having Mrs. Collum and Bella on his left, and James and Matilda opposite to them.

James was the first to open conversation, by the remark to Mrs. Collum, across the table, that they were "having another dull Sunday."

"That," rejoined the uncompromising lady, "seems to me a highly improper remark, sir."

"My friend Jauncy," explained Leander, in defence of his abashed companion, "was not alluding to present company, I'm sure. He meant the dulness *outside*—the fog, and so on."

"I knew it," she said; "and I repeat that it is improper and irreverent to speak of a dull Sunday in that tone of complaint. Haven't we all the week to be lively in?"

"And I'm sure, ma'am," said Jauncy, recovering himself, "you make the most of your time. Talking of fog, Tweddle, did you see those lines on it in to-day's *Umpire?* Very smart, I call them; regular witty."

"And do you both read a paper on Sunday mornings

with 'smart' and 'witty' lines in it?" demanded Mrs. Collum.

"I—I hadn't time this morning," said the unregenerate Leander; "but I do occasionally cast a eye over it before I get up."

Mrs. Collum groaned, and looked at her daughter reproachfully.

"I see by the *Weekly News*," said Jauncy, "you've had a burglary in your neighbourhood."

Leander let the carving-knife slip. "A burglary! What! in my neighbourhood? When?"

"Well, p'r'aps not a burglary; but a capture of two that were 'wanted' for it. It's all in to-day's *News*."

"I—I haven't seen a paper for the last two days," said Leander, his heart beating with hope. "Tell us about it!"

"Why, it isn't much to tell; but it seems that last Friday night, or early on Saturday morning, the constable on duty came upon two suspicious-looking chaps, propped up insensible against the railings in Queen Square, covered with blood, and unable to account for themselves. Whether they'd been trying to break in somewhere and been beaten off, or had quarrelled, or met with some accident, doesn't seem to be known for certain. But, anyway, they were arrested for loitering at night with housebreaking things about them; and, when they were got to the station, recognized as the men 'wanted' for shooting a policeman down at Camberwell some time back, and if it is proved against them they'll be hung, for certain."

"What were they called? Did it say?" asked Leander, eagerly.

"I forget one—something like Bradawl, I believe; the other had a lot of aliases, but he was best known as the 'Count,' from having lived a good deal abroad, and speaking broken English like a native."

Leander's spirits rose, in spite of his present anxieties. He had been going in fear and dread of the revenge of these ruffians, and they were safely locked up; they could trouble him no more. Small wonder, then, that his security in this respect made him better able to cope with minor dangers; and Bella's animosity seemed lulled, too—at least, she had not opened her mouth, except for food, since she sat down.

In his expansion, he gave himself the airs of a host. " I hope," he said, " I've served you all to your likings? Miss Parkinson, you're not getting on; allow me to offer you a little more pork."

"Thank you, Mr. Tweddle," said the implacable Bella, " but I won't trouble you. I haven't an appetite to-day—like I had at those gardens."

There was a challenge in this answer—not only to him, but to general curiosity—which, to her evident disappointment, was not taken up.

Leander turned to Jauncy. " I—I suppose you had no trouble in finding your way here?" he said.

" No," said Jauncy, "not more than usual; the streets were pretty full, and that makes it harder to get along."

" We met such quantities of soldiers," put in Bella. " Do you remember those two soldiers at Rosherwich, Mr. Tweddle? How funny they did look, dancing; didn't they? But I suppose I mustn't say anything about the dancing here, must I?"

" Since," said the poor badgered man, " you put it to me, Miss Parkinson, I must say that, considering the *day*, you know——"

" Yes," continued Mrs. Collum, severely; " surely

there are better topics for the Sabbath than—than a dancing soldier!"

"Mr. Tweddle knows why I stopped myself," said Bella. "But there, I won't tell of you—not now, at all events; so don't look like that at me!"

"There, Bella, that'll do," said her *fiancé*, suddenly awakening to the fact that she was trying to make herself disagreeable, and perhaps feeling slightly ashamed of her.

"James! I know what to say and what to leave unsaid, without tellings from you; thanks all the same. You needn't fear my saying a word about Mr. Tweddle and Ada—la, now, if I haven't gone and said it! What a stupid I am to run on so!"

"*Drop* it, Bella! Do you hear? That's enough," growled Jauncy.

Leander sat silent; he did not attempt again to turn the conversation: he knew better. Matilda seemed perfectly calm, and certainly showed no surface curiosity; but he feared that her mother intended to require explanations.

Miss Tweddle came in here with the original remark that winter had begun now in good earnest.

"Yes," said Bella. "Why, as we came along, there wasn't hardly a leaf on the trees in the squares; and yet only yesterday week, at the gardens, the trees hadn't begun to shed. Had they, Mr. Tweddle? Oh, but I forgot; you were so taken up with paying attention to Ada—— (*Well*, James! I suppose I can make a remark!)"

"I'll never take you out again, if you don't hold that tongue," he whispered savagely.

Mrs. Collum fixed her eyes on Leander, as he sat cowering on her right. "Leander Tweddle," she said, in a hissing whisper, "what is that young person talking about? Who—who is this 'Ada'? I insist upon being told."

"If you want to know, ask her," he retorted desperately.

All this by-play passed unnoticed by Miss Tweddle, who was probably too full of the cares of a hostess to pay attention to it; and, accordingly, she judged the pause that followed the fitting opportunity for a little speech.

"Mrs. Collum, ma'am," she began; "and my dearest Miss Matilda, the flower of all my lady lodgers; and you, Leandy; and Mr. Jauncy; and, though last mentioned, not intentionally so, I assure you, Miss Parkinson, my dear—I couldn't tell you how honoured I feel to see you all sitting, so friendly and cheerful, round my humble table. I hope this will be only the beginning of many more so; and I wish you all your very good healths!"

"Which, if I may answer for self and present company," said Mr. Jauncy, nobody else being able to utter a word, "we drink and reciprocate."

Leander was saved for the moment, and the dinner passed without further incident. But his aunt's vein of sentiment had been opened, and could not be staunched all at once; for when the cloth was removed, and the decanters and dishes of oranges placed upon the table, she gave a little preparatory cough and began again.

"I'm sure it isn't my wish to be ceremonial," she said; "but we're all among friends—for I should like to look upon you as a friend, if you'll let me," she added rather dubiously, to Bella. "And I don't really think there could be a better occasion for a sort of little ceremony that I've quite set my heart on. Leandy, *you* know what I mean; and you've got it with you, I know, because you were told to bring it with you."

"Miss Tweddle," interrupted Matilda, hurriedly, "not

now. I—I don't think Vidler has sent it back yet. I told you, you know——"

" That's all you know about it, young lady," she said, archly; " for I stepped in there yesterday and asked him about it, to make sure, and he told me it was delivered over the very Saturday afternoon before. So, Leandy, oblige me for once, and put it on the dear girl's finger before us all; you needn't be bashful with us, I'm sure, either of you."

"What is all this?" asked Mrs. Collum.

" Why, it's a ring, Mrs. Collum, ma'am, that belonged to my own dear aunt, though she never wore it; and her grandfather had the posy engraved on the inside of it. And I remember her telling me, before she was taken, that she'd left it to me in her will, but I wasn't to let it go out of the family. So I gave it to Leandy, to be his engagement ring; but it's had to be altered, because it was ever so much too large as it was."

" I always thought," said Mrs. Collum, " that it was the gentleman's duty to provide the ring."

" So Leandy wanted to; but I said, ' You can pay for the altering; but I'm fanciful about this, and I want to see dearest Miss Collum with my aunt's ring on.' "

" Oh, but, Miss Tweddle, can't you see?" said Matilda. " He's forgotten it; don't—don't tease him about it. . . . It must be for some other time, that's all!"

" Matilda, I'm surprised at you," said her mother. " To forget such a thing as that would be unpardonable in *any* young man. Leander Tweddle, you *cannot* have forgotten it."

" No," he said, " I've not forgotten it; but—but I haven't it about me, and I don't know as I could lay my hand on it, just at present, and that's the truth."

"*Part* of the truth," said Bella. "Oh, what deceitful things you men are! Leave me alone, James; I will speak. I won't sit by and hear poor dear Miss Collum deceived in this way. Miss Collum, ask him if that is all he knows about it. Ask him, and see what he says."

"I'm quite satisfied with what he has chosen to say already, Miss Parkinson; thank you," said Matilda.

"Then permit me to say, Miss Collum, that I'm truly sorry for you," said Bella.

"If you think so, Miss Parkinson, I suppose you must say so."

"I do say it," said Bella; "for it's a sorrowful sight to see meekness all run to poorness of spirit. You have a right to an explanation from Mr. Tweddle there; and you would insist on it, if you wasn't afraid (and with good reason) of the answer you'd get!"

At the beginning of this short colloquy Miss Tweddle, after growing very red and restless for some moments, had slipped out of the room, and came in now, trembling and out of breath, with a bonnet in her hand and a cloak over her arm.

"Miss Parkinson," she said, speaking very rapidly, "when I asked you to come here with my good friend and former lodger, I little thought that anything but friendship would come of it; and sorry I am that it has turned out otherwise. And my feelings to Mr. Jauncy are the same as ever; but—this is your bonnet, Miss Parkinson, and your cloak. And this is my house; and I shall be obliged if you'll kindly put on the ones, and walk out of the other at once!"

Bella burst into tears, and demanded from Mr. Jauncy why he had brought her there to be insulted.

"You brought it all on yourself," he said, gloomily; "you should have behaved!"

"What have I done," cried Bella, "to be told to go, as if I wasn't fit to stay?"

"I'll tell you what you've done," said Miss Tweddle. "You were asked here with Mr. Jauncy to meet my dear Leandy and his young lady, and get all four of you to know one another, and lay foundations for Friendship's flowery bonds. And from the moment you came in, though I paid no attention to it at first, you've done nothing but insinuate and hint, and try all you could to set my dear Miss Collum and her ma against my poor unoffending nephew; and I won't sit by any longer and hear it. Put on your bonnet and cloak, Miss Parkinson, and Mr. Jauncy (who knows I don't bear him any ill-feeling, whatever happens) will go home with you."

"I've said nothing," repeated Bella, "but what I'd a right to say, and what I'll stand to."

"If you don't put on those things," said Jauncy, "I shall go away myself, and leave you to follow as best you can."

"I'm putting them on," said Bella; and her hands were unsteady with passion as she tied her bonnet-strings. "Don't bully *me*, James, because I won't bear it! Mr. Tweddle, if you're a man, will you sit there and tell me you don't know that that ring is on a certain person's finger? Will you do that?"

The miserable man concluded that Ada had dis-regarded his entreaties, and told her sister all about the ring and the accursed statue. He could not see why the story should have so inflamed Bella; but her temper was always uncertain.

Everybody was looking at him, and he was expected to say something. His main idea was, that he would see how much Bella knew before committing himself.

"What have I ever done to offend you," he asked,

HER HANDS WERE UNSTEADY WITH PASSION AS SHE TIED HER
BONNET-STRINGS.   [*Page* 198.

'that you turn on me in this downright vixenish manner? I scorn to reply to your insinuations!"

"Do you want me to speak out plain? James, stand away, *if* you please. You may all think what you choose of me. *I* don't care! Perhaps if *you* were to come in and find the man who, only a week ago, had offered marriage to your youngest sister, figuring away as engaged to quite another lady, *you* wouldn't be all milk and honey, either. I'm doing right to expose him. The man who'd deceive one would deceive many, and so you'll find, Miss Collum, little as you think it."

"That's enough," said Miss Tweddle. "It's all a mistake, I'm sure, and you'll be sorry some day for having made it. Now go, Miss Parkinson, and make no more mischief!"

A light had burst in upon Leander's perturbed mind. Ada had not broken faith with him, after all. He remembered Bella's conduct during the return from Rosherwich, and understood at last to what a mistake her present wrath was due.

Here, at all events, was an accusation he could repel with dignity, with truth. Foolish and unlucky he had been—and how unlucky he still hoped Matilda might never learn—but false he was not; and she should not be allowed to believe it.

"Miss Parkinson," he said, "I've been badgered long enough. What is it you're trying to bring up against me about your sister Ada? Speak it out, and I'm ready to answer you."

"Leander," said Matilda, "I don't want to hear it from her. Only you tell me that you've been true to me, and that is quite enough."

"Matilda, you're a foolish girl, and don't know what you're talking about," said her mother. "It is not enough for *me;* so I beg, young woman, if you've anything to accuse the man who's to be my son-in-law of, you'll say it now, in my presence, and let him contradict it afterwards if he can."

"Will he contradict his knowing my sister Ada, who's one of the ladies at Madame Chenille's, in the Edgware Road, more than a twelvemonth since, and paying her attentions?" asked Bella.

"I don't deny," said Leander, "meeting her several times, and being considerably struck, in a quiet way. But that was before I met Matilda."

"You had met Matilda before last Saturday, I suppose?" sneered Bella, spitefully—"when you laid your plans to join our party to Rosherwich, and trouble my poor sister, who'd given up thinking of you."

"There you go, Bella!" said her *fiancé.* "What do you know about his plans? He'd no idea as Ada and you was to be there; and when I told him, as we were driving down, it was all I could do to prevent him jumping out of the cab."

"I'm highly flattered to hear it," said Bella. "But he didn't seem to be so afraid of Ada when they did meet; and you best know, Mr. Tweddle, the things you said to that poor trusting girl all the time you were walking and dancing and talking foolishness to her."

"I never said a word that couldn't have been spoke from the top of St. Paul's," protested Leander. "I did dance with her, I own, not to seem uncivil; but we only waltzed round twice."

"Then why did you give her a ring—an engagement ring too?" insisted Bella.

"Who saw me give her a ring?" he demanded hotly. "Do you dare to say you did? Did she ever tell you I gave her any ring? You *know* she didn't!"

"If I can't trust my own ears," said Bella, "I should like to know what I can trust. I heard you myself, in that railway carriage, ask my sister Ada not to tell any one about some ring, and I tried to get out of Ada afterwards what the secret was; but she wouldn't treat me as a sister, and be open with me. But any one with eyes in their head could guess what was between you, and all the time you an engaged man!"

"See there, now!" cried the injured hairdresser; "there's a thing to go and make all this mischief about! Matilda, Mrs. Collum, aunt, I declare to you I told the— the other young woman everything about my having formed new ties and that. I was very particular not to give rise to hopes which were only doomed to be dis- appointed. As to what Miss Parkinson says she over- heard, why, it's very likely I may have asked her sister to say nothing about a ring, and I won't deny it was the very same ring that I was to have brought here to-day; for the fact was, I had the misfortune to lose it in those very gardens, and naturally did not wish it talked about: and that's the truth, as I stand here. As for giving it away, I swear I never parted with it to no mortal woman!"

"After that, Bella," observed Mr. Jauncy, "you'd better say you're sorry you spoke, and come home with me—that's what you'd better do."

"I shall say nothing of the sort," she asserted. "I'm too much of a lady to stay where my company is not desired, and I'm ready to go as soon as you please. But if he was to talk his head off, he would never persuade me (whatever he may do other parties) that he's not been playing double; and if Ada were here you would soon see whether he would have the face to deny it. So good- night, Miss Tweddle, and sooner or later you'll find yourself undeceived in your precious nephew, take my word for it. Good-night, Miss Collum, and I'm only sorry you haven't more spirit than to put up with such treatment. James, are you going to keep me waiting any longer?"

Mr. Jauncy, with confused apologies to the company generally, hurried his betrothed off, in no very amiable mood, and showed his sense of her indiscretions by indulging in some very plain speaking on their homeward way.

As the street door shut behind them, Leander gave a deep sigh of relief.

"Matilda, my own dearest girl," he said, "now that that cockatrice has departed, tell me, you don't doubt your Leander, do you?"

"No," said Matilda, judicially, " I don't doubt you, Leander, only I do wish you'd been a little more open with me ; you might have told me you had gone to those gardens and lost the ring, instead of leaving me to hear it from that girl."

"So I might, darling," he owned ; "but I thought you'd disapprove."

"And if she's *my* daughter," observed Mrs. Collum, "she *will* disapprove."

But it was evident from Matilda's manner that the inference was incorrect ; the relief of finding Leander guiltless on the main count had blinded her to all minor shortcomings, and he had the happiness of knowing himself fully and freely forgiven.

If this could only have been the end ! But, while he was still throbbing with bliss, he heard a sound, at which his "bedded hair" started up and stood on end—the ill-omened sound of a slow and heavy footfall.

"Leandy," cried his aunt, "how strange you're looking !"

"There's some one in the passage," he said, hoarsely. "I'll go and see her. Don't any of you come out."

"Why, it's only our Jane," said his aunt; "she always treads heavy."

The steps were heard going up the stairs; then they seemed to pause half-way, and descend again. "I'll be bound she's forgot something," said Miss Tweddle. "I never knew such a head as that girl's;" and Leander began to be almost reassured.

The steps were heard in the adjoining room, which was shut off by folding doors from the one they were occupying.

"Leander," cried Matilda, "what *can* there be to look so frightened of?" and as she spoke there came a sounding solemn blow upon the folding-doors.

"I never saw the lady before in all my life!" moaned the guilty man, before the doors had time to swing back; for he knew too well who stood behind them.

And his foreboding was justified to the full. The doors yielded to the blow, and, opening wide, revealed the tall and commanding figure of the goddess; her face, thanks to Leander's pigments, glowing lifelike under her hood, and the gold ring gleaming on her outstretched hand.

"Leander," said the goddess, in her low musical accents, "come away."

"Upon my word!" cried Mrs. Collum. "*Who* is this person?"

He could not speak. There seemed to be a hammer beating on his brain, reducing it to a pulp.

"Perhaps," said Miss Tweddle—"perhaps, young lady, you'll explain what you've come for?"

The statue slowly pointed to Leander. "I come for

him," she said calmly. "He has vowed himself to me; he is mine!"

Matilda, after staring, incredulous, for some moments at the intruder, sank with a wild scream upon the sofa, and hid her face.

Leander flew to her side. "Matilda, my own," he implored, "don't be alarmed. She won't touch *you*; it's *me* she's come after."

Matilda rose and repulsed him with a sudden energy. "How dare you!" she cried, hysterically. "I see it all now: the ring, the—the cloak; *she* has had them all the time! . . . Fool that I was—silly, trusting fool!" And she broke out into violent hysterics.

"Go away at once, hypocrite!" enjoined her mother, addressing the distracted hairdresser, as he stood, dumb and impotent, before 'her. "Do you want to kill my poor child? Take yourself off!"

"For goodness' sake, go, Leandy," added his aunt. "I can't bear the sight of you!"

"Leander, I wait," said the statue. "Come!"

He stood there a moment longer, looking blankly at the two elder women as they bustled about the prostrate girl, and then he gave a bitter, defiant laugh.

His fate was too strong for him. No one was in the mood to listen to any explanation; it was all over! "I'm coming," he said to the goddess. "I may as well; I'm not wanted here."

And, with a smothered curse, he dashed blindly from the room, and out into the foggy street.

AN APPEAL

XII.

"If you did know to whom I gave the ring,
If you did know for whom I gave the ring,
And how unwillingly I left the ring,
You would abate the strength of your displeasure."
Merchant of Venice.

LEANDER strode down the street in a whirl of con-
flicting emotions. At the very moment when he seemed
to have prevailed over Miss Parkinson's machinations,
his evil fate had stepped in and undone him for ever!
What would become of him without Matilda? As he
was thinking of his gloomy prospects, he noticed, for the
first time, that the statue was keeping step by his side,
and he turned on her with smothered rage. "Well," he
began, "I hope you're satisfied?"

"Quite, Leander, quite satisfied; for have I not
found you?"

"Oh, you've found me right enough," he replied,
with a groan—"trust you for that! What I should like
to know is, how the dickens you did it?"

"Thus," she replied: "I awoke, and it was dark,
and you were not there, and I needed you; and I went
forth, and called you by your name. And you, now that
you have hearkened to my call, you are happy, are you
not?"

"Me?" said Leander, grimly. "Oh, I'm regular jolly, I am! Haven't I reason?"

"Your sisters seemed alarmed at my coming," she said. "Why?"

"Well," said Leander, "they aren't used to having marble goddesses dropping in on them promiscuously."

"The youngest wept: was it because I took you from her side?"

"I shouldn't wonder," he returned gruffly. "Don't bother me!"

When they were both safely within the little upper room again, he opened the cupboard door wide. "Now, marm," he said, in a voice which trembled with repressed rage, "you must be tired with the exercise you've took this evening, and I'll trouble you to walk in here."

"There are many things on which I would speak with you," she said.

"You must keep them for next time," he answered roughly. "If you can see anything, you can see that just now I'm not in a temper for to stand it, whatever I may be another evening."

"Why do I suffer this language from you?" she demanded indignantly—"why?"

"If you don't go in, you'll hear language you'll like still less, goddess or no goddess!" he said, foaming. "I mean it. I've been worked up past all bearing, and I advise you to let me alone just now, or you'll repent it!"

"Enough!" she said haughtily, and stalked proudly into the lonely niche, which he closed instantly. As he did so, he noticed his Sunday papers lying still folded on his table, and seized one eagerly.

"It may have something in it about what Jauncy was

telling me of," he said ; and his search was rewarded by
the following paragraph :—

"DARING CAPTURE OF BURGLARS IN BLOOMSBURY.—
On the night of Friday, the —th, Police-constable Yorke,
B 954, while on duty, in the course of one of his rounds,
discovered two men, in a fainting condition and covered
with blood, which was apparently flowing from sundry
wounds upon their persons, lying against the railings of
Queen Square. Being unable to give any coherent account of themselves, and housebreaking implements
being found in their possession, they were at once
removed to the Bow Street Station, where, the charge
having been entered against them, they were recognized
by a member of the force as two notorious housebreakers
who have long been 'wanted' in connection with the
Camberwell burglary, in which, as will be remembered,
an officer lost his life."

The paragraph went on to give their names and
sundry other details, and concluded with a sentence
which plunged Leander into fresh torments :—

"In spite of the usual caution, both prisoners insisted
upon volunteering a statement, the exact nature of which
has not yet transpired, but which is believed to have
reference to another equally mysterious outrage—the
theft of the famous Venus from the Wricklesmarsh
Collection—and is understood to divert suspicion into a
hitherto unsuspected channel."

What could this mean, if not that those villains,
smarting under their second failure, had denounced him
in revenge? He tried to persuade himself that the
passage would bear any other construction, but not very
successfully. "If they have brought *me* in," he thought,
and it was his only gleam of consolation, "I should have
heard of it before this."

And even this gleam vanished as a sharp knocking was heard below ; and, descending to open the door, he found his visitor to be Inspector Bilbow.

"Evening, Tweddle," said the Inspector, quietly. "I've come to have another little talk with you."

Leander thought he would play his part till it became quite hopeless. "Proud to see you, Mr. Inspector," he said. "Will you walk into my saloon ? and I'll light the gas for you."

"No, don't you trouble yourself," said the terrible man. "I'll walk upstairs where you're sitting yourself, if you've no objections."

Leander dared not make any, and he ushered the detective upstairs accordingly.

"Ha !" said the latter, throwing a quick eye round the little room. "Nice little crib you've got here. Keep everything you want on the premises, eh ? Find those cupboards very convenient, I dare say ?"

"Very," said Leander (like the innocent Joseph Surface that he was) ; "oh, very convenient, sir." He tried to keep his eyes from resting too consciously upon the fatal door that held his secret.

"Keep your coal and your wine and spirits there ?" said the detective. (Was he watching his countenance, or not ?)

"Y—yes," said Leander ; "leastways, in one of them. Will you take anything, sir ?"

"Thank 'ee, Tweddle ; I don't mind if I do. And what do you keep in the other one, now ?"

"The other ?" said the poor man. "Oh, odd things !" (He certainly had *one* odd thing in it.)

After the officer had chosen and mixed his spirits and water, he began : "Now, you know what's brought me here, don't you ?"

("If he was sure, he wouldn't try to pump me," argued Leander. "I won't throw up just yet.")

"I suppose it's the ring," he replied innocently. "You don't mean to say you've got it back for me, Mr. Inspector? Well, I *am* glad."

"I thought you set no particular value on the ring when I met you last?" said the other.

"Why," said Leander, "I may have said so out of politeness, not wanting to trouble you; but, as you said it was the statue you were after chiefly, why, I don't mind admitting that I shall be thankful indeed to get that ring back. And so you've brought it, have you, sir?"

He said this so naturally, having called in all his powers of dissimulation to help him in his extremity, that the detective was favourably impressed. He had already felt a suspicion that he had been sent here on a fool's errand, and no one could have looked less like a daring criminal, and the trusted confederate of still more daring ruffians, than did Leander at that moment.

"Heard anything of Potter lately?" he asked, wishing to try the effect of a sudden *coup*.

"I don't know the gentleman," said Leander, firmly; for, after all, he did not.

"Now, take care. He's been seen to frequent this house. We know more than you think, young man."

"Oh! if he bluffs, *I* can bluff too," passed through Leander's mind. "Inspector Bilbow," he said, "I give you my sacred honour, I've never set eyes on him. He can't have been here, not with my knowledge. It's my belief you're trying to make out something against me. If you're a friend, Inspector, you'll tell me straight out."

"That's not our way of doing business; and yet, hang it, I ought to know an honest man by this time! Tweddle, I'll drop the investigator, and speak as man to man.

You've been reported to me (never mind by whom) as the receiver of the stolen Venus—a pal of this very Potter—that's what I've against you, my man!"

"I know who told you that," said Leander; "it was that Count and his precious friend Braddle!"

"Oh, you know them, do you? That's an odd guess for an innocent man, Tweddle!"

"They found me out from inquiries at the gardens," said Leander; "and as for guessing, it's in this very paper. So it's me they've gone and implicated, have they? All right. I suppose they're men whose word you'd go by, wouldn't you, sir—truthful, reliable kind of parties, eh?"

"None of that, Tweddle," said the Inspector, rather uneasily. "We officers are bound to follow up any clue, no matter where it comes from. I was informed that that Venus is concealed somewhere about these premises. It may be, or it may not be; but it's my duty to make the proper investigations. If you were a prince of the blood, it would be all the same."

"Well, all I can say is, that I'm as innocent as my own toilet preparations. Ask yourself if it is likely. What could *I* do with a stolen statue—not to mention that I'm a respectable tradesman, with a reputation to maintain? Excuse me, but I'm afraid those burglars have been 'aving a lark with you, sir."

He went just a little too far here, for the detective was visibly irritated.

"Don't chatter to me," he said. "If you're innocent, so much the better for you; if that statue is found here after this, it will ruin you. If you know anything, be it ever so little, about it, the best thing you can do is to speak out while there's time."

"I can only say, once more, I'm as innocent as the

drivelling snow," repeated Leander. "Why can't you believe my word against those blackguards?"

"Perhaps I do," said the other; "but I must make a formal look round, to ease my conscience."

Leander's composure nearly failed him. "By all means," he said at length. "Come and ease your conscience all over the house, sir, do; I can show you over."

"Softly," said the detective. "I'll begin here, and work gradually up, and then down again."

"Here?" said Leander, aghast. "Why, you've seen all there is there!"

"Now, Tweddle, I shall conduct this my own way, if *you* please. I've been following your eyes, Tweddle, and they've told me tales. I'll trouble you to open that cupboard you keep looking at so."

"This cupboard?" cried Leander. "Why, you don't suppose I've got the Venus in there, sir!"

"If it's anywhere, it's there! There's no taking me in, I tell you. Open it!"

"Oh!" said Leander, "it is hard to be the object of these cruel suspicions. Mr. Inspector, listen to me. I can't open that cupboard, and I'll tell you why. . . . You—you've been young yourself. . . . Think how you'd feel in my situation . . . and consider *her!* As a gentleman, you won't press it, I'm sure!"

"If I'm making any mistake, I shall know how to apologise," said the Inspector. "If you don't open that cupboard, *I* shall."

"Never!" exclaimed Leander. "I'll die first!" and he threw himself upon the handle.

The other caught him by the shoulders, and sent him twirling into the opposite corner; and then, taking a key from his own pocket, he opened the door himself.

"I—I never encouraged her!" whimpered Leander, as he saw that all was lost.

The officer had stepped back in silence from the cupboard; then he faced Leander, with a changed expression. "I suppose you think yourself devilish sharp?" he said savagely; and Leander discovered that the cupboard was as bare as Mother Hubbard's!

He was not precisely surprised, except at first. "She's keeping out of the way; she wouldn't be the goddess she is if she couldn't do a trifling thing like that!" was all he thought of the phenomenon. He forced himself to laugh a little.

"Excuse me," he said, "but you did seem so set on detecting something wrong, that I couldn't help humouring you!"

Inspector Bilbow was considerably out of humour, and gave Leander to understand that he would laugh in a certain obscure region, known as "the other side of his face," by-and-by. "You take care, that's my advice to you, young man. I've a deuced good mind to arrest you on suspicion as it is!" he said hotly.

"Lor', sir!" said Leander, "what for—for not having anything in that cupboard?"

"It's my belief you know more than you choose to tell. Be that as it may, I shall not take you into custody for the present; but you pay attention to what I'm going to tell you next. Don't you attempt to leave this house, or to remove anything from it, till you see me again, and that'll be some time to-morrow evening. If you do attempt it, you'll be apprehended at once, for you're being watched. I tell you that for your own sake, Tweddle; for I've no wish to get you into trouble if you act fairly by me. But mind you stay where you are for the next twenty-four hours."

" And what's to happen then ? " said Leander.

" I mean to have the whole house thoroughly searched
and you must be ready to give us every assistance—that's
what's to happen. I might make a secret of it; but
where's the use? If you're not a fool, you'll see that it
won't do to play any tricks. You'd far better stand by
me than Potter."

" I tell you I don't know Potter. *Blow* Potter !" said
Leander, warmly.

" We shall see," was all the detective deigned to
reply; " and just be ready for my men to-morrow evening, or take the consequences. Those are my last words
to you ! "

And with this he took his leave. He was by no means
the most brilliant officer in the Department, and he felt
uncomfortably aware that he did not see his way clear
as yet. He could not even make up his mind on so
elementary a point as Leander's guilt or innocence.

But he meant to take the course he had announced,
and his frankness in giving previous notice was not without calculation. He argued thus : If Tweddle was free
from all complicity, nothing was lost by delaying the
search for a day; if he were guilty, he would be more
than mortal if he did not attempt, after such a warning,
either to hide his booty more securely, and probably
leave traces which would betray him, or else to escape
when his guilt would be manifest.

Unfortunately, there were circumstances in the case
which he could not be expected to know, and which
made his logic inapplicable.

After he had gone, Leander thrust his hands deep
into his pockets, and began to whistle forlornly. " A
little while ago it was burglars—now it's police !" he
reflected aloud. " I'm going it, I am ! And then there's

Matilda and that there Venus—one predickyment on top of another!" (But here a sudden hope lightened his burden.) "Suppose she's took herself off for good?" He was prevented from indulging this any further by a long, low laugh, which came from the closed cupboard.

"No such luck—she's back again!" he groaned. "Oh, *come* out if you want to. Don't stay larfin' at me in there!"

The goddess stepped out, with a smile of subdued mirth upon her lips. "Leander," she said, "did it surprise you just now that I had vanished?"

"Oh," he said wearily, "I don't know—yes, I suppose so. You found some way of getting through at the back, I dare say?"

"Do you think that even now I cannot break through the petty restraints of matter?"

"Well, however it was managed, it was cleverly done. I must say that. I didn't hardly expect it of you. But you must do the same to-morrow night, mind you!"

"Must I, indeed?" she said.

"Yes, unless you want to ruin me altogether, you must. They're going to search the premises *for you!*"

"I have heard all," she said. "But give yourself no anxiety: by that time you and I will be beyond human reach."

"Not me," he corrected. "If you think I'm going to let myself be wafted over to Cyprus (which is British soil now, let me tell you), you're under a entire delusion. I've never been wafted anywhere yet, and I don't mean to try it!"

All her pent-up wrath broke forth and descended upon him with crushing force.

"Meanest and most contemptible of mortal men, you shall recognize me as the goddess I am! I have borne

LEANDER WENT DOWN ON ALL FOURS ON THE HEARTHRUG.

[*Page* 221.

with you too long ; it shall end this night. Shallow fool
that you have been, to match your puny intellect against
a goddess famed for her wiles as for her beauty ! You
have thought me simple and guileless ; you have never
feared to treat me with disrespect ; you have even
dared to suppose that you could keep me—an immortal
—pent within these wretched walls ! I humoured you,
I let you fool yourself with the notion that your will was
free—your soul your own. Now that is over ! Consider
the perils which encircle you. Everything has been
aiding to drive you into these arms. My hour of triumph
is at hand—yield, then ! Cast yourself at my feet, and
grovel for pardon—for mercy—or assuredly I will spare
you not ! "

Leander went down on all fours on the hearthrug.
" Mercy ! " he cried, feebly. " I've meant no offence.
Only tell me what you want of me."

" Why should I tell you again ? I demand the words
from you which place you within my power : speak them
at once ! "

(" Ah," thought Leander, " I am not in her power
as it is, then.") " If I was to tell you once more that I
couldn't undertake to say any such words ? " he asked
aloud.

" Then," she said, " my patience would be at an end,
and I would scatter your vile frame to the four winds of
heaven ! "

" Lady Venus," said Leander, getting up with a white
and desperate face, " don't drive me into a corner. I
can't go off, not at a moment's notice—in either way !
I—I must have a day—only a day—to make my arrangements in. Give me a day, Lady Venus ; I ask it as a
partickler favour ! "

" Be it so," she said. " One day I give you in which

to take leave of such as may be dear to you; but, after that, I will listen to no further pleadings. You are mine, and, all unworthy as you are, I shall hold you to your pledge!"

Leander was left with this terrible warning ringing in his ears: the goddess would hold him to his involuntary pledge. Even he could see that it was pride, and not affection, which rendered her so determined; and he trembled at the thought of placing himself irrevocably in her power.

But what was he to do? The alternative was too awful; and then, in either case, he must lose Matilda. Here the recollection of how he had left her came over him with a vivid force. What must she be thinking of him at that moment? And who would ever tell her the truth, when he had been spirited away for ever?

"Oh, Matilda!" he cried, "if you only knew the hidgeous position I'm in—if you could only advise me what to do—I could bear it better!"

And then he resolved that he would ask that advice without delay, and decide nothing until she replied. There was no reason for any further concealment: she had seen the statue herself, and must know the worst. What she could not know was his perfect innocence of any real unfaithfulness to her, and that he must explain.

He sat up all night composing a letter that should touch her to the heart, with the following result:—

"My own dearest Girl,

"If such you will still allow me to qualify you, I write to you in a state of mind that I really ardly know what I am about, but I cannot indure making no effort to clear up the gaping abiss which the events of the past fatal afternoon has raised betwixt us.

"In spite of all I could do, you have now seen, and been justly alarmed at, the Person with whom I allowed myself to become involved in such a unhappy and unprecedented manner, and having done so, you can think for yourself whether that Art of Stone was able for to supplant yours for a single moment, though the way in which such a hidgeous Event transpired I can not trust my pen to describe except in the remark that it was purely axidental. It all appened on that ill-ominous Saturday when we went down to those Gardens where my Doom was saving up to lay in wait for me, and I scorn to deny that Bella's sister Ada was one of the party. But as to anything serous in that quarter, oh Tilly the ole time I was contrasting you with her and thinking how truly superior, and never did I swerve not what could be termed a swerve for a instant. I did dance arf a walz with her—but why? Because she asked me to it and as a Gentleman I was bound to oblige! And that was afterwards too, when I had put that ring on which is the sauce of all my recent aggony. All the while I was dancing my thoughts were elsewhere —on how I could get the ring back again, for so I still hoped I could, though when I came to have a try, oh my dear girl no one couldn't persuade her she's that obstinate, and yet unless I do it is all over with me, and soon too!

"And now if it's the last time I shall ever write words with a mortal pen, I must request your support in this dilemmer which is sounding its dread orns at my very door!

"You know what she is and who she is, and you cannot doubt but what she's a *godess* loath as you must feel to admit such a thing, and I ask you if it would be downright wicked in me to do what she tells me I must do. Indeed I wont do it, being no less than flying with her immediate to a distant climb, and you know how repugnant I am to such a action—not if you advise me against it or even if you was but to assure me your affections were unchanged in spite of all! But you know we parted under pigulier circs, and I cannot disgise from myself that you may be thinking wuss of me than what Matilda I can honestly say I deserve!

"Now I tell you solimly that if this is the fact, and you've been thinking of your proper pride and your womanly dignity and things like that—there's *no time for to do it in* Matilda, if you don't want to break with me for all Eternity!

"For she's pressing me to carry out the pledge, as she calls it, and I must decide before this time to-morrow, and I want to feel you are not lost to me before I can support my trial, and what with countless perplexities and burglars threatening, and giving false informations, and police searching, there's no saying what I may do nor what I mayn't do if I'm left to myself, for indeed I am very unappy Matilda, and if ever a man was made a Victim through acting without intentions, or if with, of the best—I am that Party! O Matilda don't, don't desert me, unless you have seased to care for me, and in that contingency I can look upon my Fate whatever it be with a apathy that will supply the courage which will not even winch at its approach, but if I am still of value, come, and come precious soon, or it will be too late to the Asistance of

"Your truly penitent and unfortunate

"LEANDER TWEDDLE.

"P.S.—You will see the condition of my feelings from my spelling—I haven't the hart to spell."

Dawn was breaking as he put the final touches to this appeal, and read it over with a gloomy approbation. He had always cherished the conviction that he could " write a good letter when he was put to it," and felt now that he had more than risen to the occasion.

" William shall take it down to Bayswater the first thing to-morrow—no, to-day, I mean," he said, rubbing his hot eyes. " I fancy it will do my business ! "

And it did.

THE LAST STRAW

XIII.

"Thou in justice,
If from the height of majesty we can
Look down upon thy lowness and embrace it,
Art bound with fervour to look up to me."

MASSINGER, *Roman Actor.*

HAGGARD and distraught was Leander as he went about his business that morning, so mechanically that one customer, who had requested to have his luxuriant locks "trimmed," found himself reduced to a state of penal bullet-headedness before he could protest, and another sacrificed his whiskers and part of one ear to the hairdresser's uninspired scissors. For Leander's eyes were constantly turning to the front part of his shop, where his apprentice might come in at any moment with the answer to his appeal.

At last the moment came when the bell fixed at the door sounded sharply, and he saw the sleek head and chubby red face he had been so anxiously expecting. He was busy with a customer; but that could not detain him then, and he rushed quickly into the outer shop. "Well, William," he said, breathlessly, "a nice time you've been over that message! I gave you the money for your 'bus."

" Yusser, but it was this way : you said a green 'bus,

and I took a green 'bus with 'Bayswater' on it, and I didn't know nothing was wrong, and when it stopped I sez to the conductor, 'This ain't Kensington Gardings;' and he sez, 'No, it's Archer Street;' and I sez—— "

" Never mind that now; you got to the shop, didn't you? "

" Yes, I got to the shop, sir, and I see the lady; but I sez to that conductor, 'You should ha' told me,' I sez—— "

" Did she give you anything for me? " interrupted Leander, impatiently.

" Yessur," said the boy.

" Then where the dooce is it? "

" 'Ere!" said William, and brought out an envelope, which his master tore open with joy. It contained his own letter!

" William," he said unsteadily, " is this all? "

" Ain't it enough, sir? " said the young scoundrel, who had guessed the state of affairs, and felt an impish satisfaction at his employer's rejection.

" None of that, William; d'ye hear me? " said Leander. " William, I ain't been a bad master to you. Tell me, how did she take it? "

" Well," she didn't seem to want to take it nohow at first," said the boy. " I went up to the desk where she was a-sittin' and gave it her, and by-and-by she opened it with the tips of her fingers, as if it would bite, and read it all through very careful, and I could see her nose going up gradual, and her colour coming, and then she sez to me, 'You may go now, boy; there's no answer.' And I sez to her, 'If you please, miss, master said as I was not to go away without a answer.' So she sez, uncommon short and stiff, 'In that case he shall have it!'— like that, she says, as proud as a queen, and she scribbles a line or two on it, and throws it to me, and goes on casting up figgers."

"A line or two! where?" cried Leander, and caught up the letter again. Yes, there on the last page was Matilda's delicate commercial handwriting, and the poor man read the cruel words, "*I have nothing to advise; I give you up to your 'goddess!'*"

"Very well, William," he said, with a deadly calm; "that's all. You young devil! what are you a-sniggering at?" he added, with a sudden outburst.

"On'y something I 'eard a boy say in the street, sir, going along, sir; nothing to do with you, sir."

"Oh, youth, youth!" muttered the poor broken man; "boys don't grow feelings, any more than they grow whiskers!"

And he went back to his saloon, where he was instantly hailed with reproaches from the abandoned customer.

"Look here, sir! what do you mean by this? I told you I wanted to be shaved, and you've soaped the top of my head and left it to cool! What"—and he made use of expletives here—"what are you about?"

Leander apologized on the ground of business of a pressing nature, but the customer was not pacified.

"Business, sir! your business is *here: I'm* your business! And I come to be shaved, and you soap the top of my head, and leave me all alone to dry! It's scandalous! it's—— "

"Look here, sir," interrupted Leander, gloomily; "I've a good deal of private trouble to put up with just now, without having *you* going on at me; so I must ask you not to 'arris me like this, or I don't know what I might do, with a razor so 'andy!"

"That'll do!" said the customer, hastily. "I—I

don't care about being shaved this morning. Wipe my
head, and let me go; no, I'll wipe it myself,—don't you
trouble!" and he made for the door. "It's my belief,"
he said, pausing on the threshold for an instant, "that
you're a dangerous lunatic, sir; you ought to be shut up!"

"I dessay I shall have a mad doctor down on me
after this," thought Leander; "but I shan't wait for *him*.
No, it is all over now; the die is fixed! Cruel Tillie!
you have spoke the mandrake; you have thrust me into
the stony harms of that 'cathen goddess—always supposing the police don't nip in fust, and get the start of
her."

No more customers came that day, which was fortunate, perhaps, for them. The afternoon passed, and
dusk approached, but the hairdresser sat on, motionless,
in his darkening saloon, without the energy to light a
single gas-jet.

At last he roused himself sufficiently to go to the
head of the stairs leading to his "labatry," and call for
William, who, it appeared, was composing an egg-wash,
after one of his employer's formulæ, and came up,
wondering to find the place in darkness.

"Come here, William," said Leander, solemnly. "I
just want a few words with you, and then you can go.
I can do the shutting-up myself. William, we can none
of us foretell the future; and it may so 'appen that you
are looking on my face for the last time. If it should so
be, William, remember the words I am now about to
speak, and lay them to 'art! . . . This world is full of
pitfalls; and some of us walk circumspect and keep out
of 'em, and some of us, William—some of us don't. If
there's any places more abounding in pitfalls than what
others are, it is the noxious localities known under the
deceitful appellation of 'pleasure' gardens. And you

may take that as the voice of one calling to you from the bottom of about as deep a 'ole as a mortal man ever plumped into. And if ever you find a taste for statuary growing on you, William, keep it down, wrastle with it, and don't encourage it. Farewell, William! Be here at the usual time to-morrow, though whether you will find *me* here is more than I can say."

The boy went away, much impressed by so elaborate and formal a parting, which seemed to him a sign that, in his parlance, "the guv'nor was going to make a bolt of it."

Leander busied himself in some melancholy preparations for his impending departure, dissolution, or incarceration; he was not very clear which it might be.

He went down and put his "labatry" in order. There he had worked with all the fiery zeal of an inventor at the discoveries which were to confer perpetual youth, in various sized bottles, upon a grateful world. He must leave them all, with his work scarcely begun! Another would step in and perfect what he had left incomplete!

He came up again, with a heavy heart, and examined his till. There was not much; enough, however, for William's wages and any small debts. He made a list of these, and left it there with the coin. "They must settle it among themselves," he thought, wearily; "I can't be bothered with business now."

He was thinking whether it was worth while to shut the shop up or not; when a clear voice sounded from above—

"Leander, where art thou? Come hither!"

And he started as if he had been shot. "I'm coming, madam," he called up, obsequiously. "I'll be with you in one minute!"

"Now for it," he thought, as he went up to his sitting-room. "I wish I wasn't all of a twitter. I wish I knew what was coming next!"

The room was dark, but when he got a light he saw the statue standing in the centre of the room, her hood thrown back, and the fur-lined mantle hanging loosely about her; the face looked stern and terrible under its brilliant tint.

"Have you made your choice?" she demanded.

"Choice!" he said. I haven't any choice left me!"

"It is true," she said triumphantly. "Your friends have deserted you; mortals are banded together to seize and disgrace you: you have no refuge but with me. But time is short. Come, then, place yourself within the shelter of these arms, and, while they enfold you tight in their marble embrace, repeat after me the words which complete my power."

"There's no partickler hurry," he objected. "I will directly. I—I only want to know what will happen when I've done it. You can't have any objection to a natural curiosity like that."

"You will lose consciousness, to recover it in balmy Cyprus, with Aphrodite (no longer cold marble, but the actual goddess, warm and living), by your side! Ah! impervious one, can you linger still? Do you not tremble with haste to feel my breath fanning your cheek, my soft arm around your neck? Are not your eyes already dazzled by the gleam of my golden tresses?"

"Well, I can't say they are; not at present," said Leander. "And, you see, it's all very well; but, as I asked you once before, how are you going to *get* me there? It's a long way, and I'm ten stone, if I'm an ounce!"

" Heavy-witted youth, it is not your body that will taste perennial bliss."

" And what's to become of that, then ? " he asked, anxiously.

" That will be left here, clasped to this stone, itself as cold and lifeless."

" Oh ! " said Leander, " I didn't bargain for that, and I don't like it."

" You will know nothing of it ; you will be with me, in dreamy grottoes strewn with fragrant rushes and the new-stript leaves of the vine, where the warm air woos to repose with its languorous softness, and the water as it wells murmurs its liquid laughter. Ah ! no Greek would have hesitated thus."

" Well, I ain't a Greek ; and, as a business man, you can't be surprised if I want to make sure it's a genuine thing, and worth the risk, before I commit myself. I think I understand that it's the gold ring which is to bind us two together ? "

" It is," she said ; " by that pure and noble metal are we united."

" Well," said Leander, " that being so, I should wish to have it tested, else there might be a hitch somewhere or other."

" Tested ! " she cried ; " what is that ? "

" Trying it, to see if it's real gold or not," he said. " We can easily have it done."

" It is needless," she replied, haughtily. " I will not suffer my power to be thus doubted, nor that of the pure and precious metal through which I have obtained it ! "

Leander might have objected to this as an example of that obscure feat, " begging the question ; " for, whether the metal *was* pure and precious, was precisely the point he desired to ascertain. And this desire was quite genuine; for, though he saw no other course before him but that upon which the goddess insisted, he did wish to take every reasonable precaution.

"For all I know," he reasoned in his own mind, "if there's anything wrong with that ring, I may be left 'igh and dry, halfway to Cyprus; or she may get tired of me, and turn me out of those grottoes of hers! If I must go with her, I should like to make things as safe as I could."

"It won't take long," he pleaded; "and if I find the ring's real gold, I promise I won't hold out any longer."

"There is no time," she said, "to indulge this whim. Would you mock me, Leander? Ha! did I not say so? Listen!"

The private bell was ringing loudly. Leander rushed to the window, but saw no one. Then he heard the clang of the shop bell, as if the person or persons had discovered that an entrance was possible there.

"The guards!" said the statue. "Will you wait for them, Leander?"

"No!" he cried. "Never mind what I said about the ring; I'll risk that. Only—only, don't go away without me. . . . Tell me what to say, and I'll say it, and chance the consequences!"

"Say, 'Aphrodite, daughter of Olympian Zeus, I yield; I fulfil the pledge; I am thine!"

"Well," he thought, "here goes. Oh, Matilda, you're responsible for this!" And he advanced towards the white extended arms of the goddess. There were hasty steps outside; another moment and the door would be burst open.

"Aphrodite, daughter of——" he began, and recoiled suddenly; for he heard his name called from without in a voice familiar and once dear to him.

"Leander, where are you? It's all dark! Speak to

"STOP WHERE YOU ARE! . . . FOR MERCY'S SAKE, DON'T
COME IN!"   [*Page* 239.

me; tell me you've done nothing rash! Oh, Leander, it's Matilda!"

That voice, which a short while back he would have given the world to hear once more, appalled him now. For if she came in, the goddess would discover who she was, and then—he shuddered to think what might happen then!

Matilda's hand was actually on the door. "Stop where you are!" he shouted, in despair; "for mercy's sake, don't come in!"

"Ah! you are there, and alive!" she cried. "I am not too late; and I *will* come in!"

And in another instant she burst into the room, and stood there, her tear-stained face convulsed with the horror of finding him in such company.

THE THIRTEENTH TRUMP

XIV.

"Your adversary having thus secured the lead with the last trump, you will be powerless to prevent the bringing-in of the long suit."

Rough's *Guide to Whist.*

"What! thinkest thou that utterly in vain
Jove is my sire, and in despite my will
That thou canst mock me with thy beauty still?"

Story of Cupid and Psyche.

LEANDER, when he wrote his distracted appeal to Matilda, took it for granted that she had recognized the statue for something of a supernatural order, and this, combined with his perplexed state of mind, caused him to be less explicit than he might have been in referring to the goddess's ill-timed appearance.

But, unfortunately, as will probably have been already anticipated, the only result of this reticence was, that Matilda saw in his letter an abject entreaty for her consent to his marriage with Ada Parkinson, to avoid legal proceedings, and, under this misapprehension, she wrote the line that abandoned all claims upon him, and then went on with her accounts, which were not so neatly kept that day as usual.

What she felt most keenly in Leander's conduct was, that he should have placed the ring, which to all intent was her own, upon the finger of another. She could not bear to think of so unfeeling an act, and yet she thought of it all through the long day, as she sat, outwardly serene, at her high desk, while her attendants at her side made up sprays for dances and wreaths for funerals from the same flowers.

And at last she felt herself urged to a course which, in her ordinary mind, she would have shrunk from as a lowering of her personal dignity : she would go and see her rival, and insist that this particular humiliation should be spared her. The ring was not Leander's to dispose of—at least, to dispose of thus ; it was not right that any but herself should wear it ; and, though the token could never now be devoted to its rightful use, she wanted to save it from what, in her eyes, was a kind of profanation.

She would not own it to herself, but there was a motive stronger than all this—the desire to relieve her breast of some of the indignation which was choking her, and of which her pride forbade any betrayal to Leander himself.

This other woman had supplanted her ; but she should be made to feel the wrong she had done, and her triumphs should be tempered with shame, if she were capable of such a sensation. Matilda knew very well that the ring was not hers, and she wanted it no longer ; but, then, it was Miss Tweddle's, and she would claim it in her name.

She easily obtained permission to leave somewhat earlier that evening, as she did not often ask such favours, and soon found herself at Madame Chenille's establishment, where she remembered to have heard from Bella that her sister was employed.

She asked for the forewoman, and begged to be allowed to speak to Miss Parkinson in private for a very

few minutes ; but the forewoman referred her to the pro-
prietress, who made objections : such a thing was never
permitted during business hours, the shop would close in
an hour, till then Miss Parkinson was engaged in the
show-room, and so on.

But Matilda carried her point at last, and was shown
to a room in the basement, where the assistants took
their meals, there to wait until Miss Parkinson could be
spared from her duties.

Matilda waited in the low, dingy room, where the tea-
things were still littering the table, and as she paced
restlessly about, trying to feel an interest in the long-
discarded fashion-plates which adorned the walls, her
anger began to cool, and give place to something very
like nervousness.

She wished she had not come. What, after all, was
she to say to this girl when they met ? And what was
Leander—base and unworthy as he had shown himself—
to her any longer ? Why should she care what he chose
to do with the ring ? And he would be told of her visit,
and think—— No ! that was intolerable : she would not
gratify his vanity and humble herself in this way. She
would slip quietly out, and leave her rival to enjoy her
victory !

But, just as she was going to carry out this intention,
the door opened, and a short, dark young woman
appeared. " I'm told there was a young person asking
to speak to me," she said ; " I'm Ada Parkinson."

At the name, Matilda's heart swelled again with the
sense of her injuries ; and yet she was unprepared for
the face that met her eyes. Surely her rival had both
looked and spoken differently the night before ? And
yet, she had been so agitated that very likely her recollections were not to depended upon.

245

" I—I did want to see you," she said, and her voice shook, as much from timidity as righteous indignation. " When I tell you who I am, perhaps you will guess why. I am Matilda Collum."

Miss Parkinson showed no symptoms of remorse. " What!" she cried, " the young lady that Mr. Tweddle is courting? Fancy ! "

"After what happened last night," said Matilda, trembling exceedingly, " you know that that is all over. I didn't come to talk about that. If you knew—and I think you must have known—all that Mr. Tweddle was to me, you have—you have not behaved very well; but he is nothing to me any more, and it is not worth while to be angry. Only, I don't think you ought to keep the ring—not *that* ring ! "

" Goodness gracious me !" cried Ada. " What in the world is all this about? What ring oughtn't I to keep ? "

" You know !" retorted Matilda. " How can you pretend like that ? The ring he gave you that night at Rosherwich ! "

" The girl's mad !" exclaimed the other. " He never gave me a ring in all his life ! I wouldn't have taken it, if he'd asked me ever so. Mr. Tweddle indeed ! "

" Why do you say that?" said Matilda. " He has not got it himself, and your sister said he gave it to you , and—and I saw it with my own eyes on your hand ! "

" Oh, *dear* me !" said Ada, petulantly, holding out her hand, " look there—is that it?—is this? Well, these are all that I have, whether you believe me or not; one belonged to my poor mother, and the other was a present, only last Friday, from the gentleman that's their head traveller, next door, and is going to be my husband. Is it likely that I should be wearing any other now?—ask yourself!"

"You wouldn't wish to deceive me, I hope," said Matilda; "and oh, Miss Parkinson, you might be open with me, for I'm so very miserable! I don't know what to think. Tell me just this: did you—wasn't it you who came last night to Miss Tweddle's?"

"No!" returned Ada, impatiently—"no, as many times as you please! And if Bella likes to say I did, she may; and she always was a mischief-making thing! How could I, when I didn't know there was any Miss Tweddle to come to? And what do you suppose I should go running about after Mr. Tweddle for? I wonder you're not ashamed to say such things!"

"But," faltered Matilda, "you did go to those gardens with him, didn't you? And—and I know he gave the ring to somebody!"

Ada began to laugh. "You're quite correct, Miss Collum," she said; "so he did. Don't you want to know who he gave it to?"

"Yes," said Matilda, "and you will tell me. I have a right to be told. I was engaged to him, and the ring was given to him for me—not for any one else. You *will* tell me, Miss Parkinson, I am sure you will?"

"Well," said Ada, still laughing, "I'll tell you this much—she's a foreign lady, very stiff and stuck-up and cold. She's got it, if any one has. I saw him put it on myself!"

"Tell me her name, if you know it."

"I see you won't be easy till you know all about it. Her name's Afriddity, or Froddity, or something outlandish like that. She lives at Rosherwich, a good deal in the open air, and—there, don't be ridiculous—it's only a *statue!* There's a pretty thing to be jealous of!"

247

"Only a statue!" echoed Matilda. "Oh! Heaven be with us both, if—if that was It!"

Certain sentences in the letter she had returned came to her mind with a new and dreadful significance. The appearance of the visitor last night—Leander's terror— all seemed to point to some unsuspected mystery.

"It can't be—no, it can't! Miss Parkinson, you were there: tell me all that happened, quick! You don't know what may depend on it!"

"What! not satisfied even now?" cried Ada. " *Well*, Miss Collum, talk about jealousy! But, there, I'll tell you all I know myself."

And she gave the whole account of the episode with the statue, so far as she knew it, even to the conversation which led to the production of the ring.

"You see," she concluded, "that it was all on your account that he tried it on at all, and I'm sure he talked enough about you all the evening. I really was a little surprised when I found *you* were his Miss Collum. (You won't mind my saying so?) If I was you, I should go and tell him I forgave him, now. I do think he deserves it, poor little man!"

"Yes, yes!" cried Matilda; "I'll go—I'll go at once! Thank you, Miss Parkinson, for telling me what you have!" And then, as she remembered some dark hints in Leander's letter: "Oh, I must make haste! He may be going to do something desperate—he may have done it already!"

And, leaving Miss Parkinson to speculate as she pleased concerning her eccentricity, she went out into the broad street again; and, unaccustomed as she was to such expenditure, hailed a hansom; for there was no time to be lost.

She had told the man to drive to the Southampton

Row Passage at first, but, as she drew nearer, she changed her purpose; she did not like to go alone, for who knew what she might see there? It was out of the question to expect her mother to accompany her, but her friend and landlady would not refuse to do so; and she drove to Millman Street, and prevailed on Miss Tweddle to come with her without a moment's delay.

The two women found the shop dark, but unshuttered; there was a light in the upper room. "You stay down here, please," said Matilda; "if—if anything is wrong, I will call you." And Miss Tweddle, without very well understanding what it was all about, and feeling fluttered and out of breath, was willing enough to sit down in the saloon and recover herself.

And so it came to pass that Matilda burst into the room just as the hairdresser was preparing to pronounce the inevitable words that would complete the goddess's power. He stood there, pale and dishevelled, with eyes that were wild and bordered with red. Opposite to him was the being she had once mistaken for a fellow-creature.

Too well she saw now that the tall and queenly form, with the fixed eyes and cold tinted mask, was inspired by nothing human; and her heart died within her as she gazed, spellbound, upon her formidable rival.

"Leander," she murmured, supporting herself against the frame of the door, "what are you going to do?"

"Keep back, Matilda!" he cried desperately; "go away—it's too late now!"

A moment before, and, deserted as he believed himself to be by love and fortune alike, he had been almost resigned to the strange and shadowy future which lay before him; but now—now that he saw Matilda there in his room, no longer scornful or indifferent, but pale and concerned, her pretty grey eyes dark and wide with anguish and fear for him—he felt all he was giving up; he had a sudden revulsion, a violent repugnance to his doom.

She loved him still! She had repented for some reason. Oh! why had she not done so before? What could he do now? For her own sake he must steel himself to tell her to leave him to his fate; for he knew well that if the goddess were to discover Matilda's real relations to him, it might cost his innocent darling her life!

For the moment he rose above his ordinary level. He lost all thought of self. Let Aphrodite take him if she would, but Matilda must be saved. "Go away!" he repeated; and his voice was cracked and harsh, under the strain of doing such violence to his feelings. "Can't you see you're—you're not wanted? Oh, do go away—while you can!"

Matilda closed the door behind her. "Do you think," she said, catching her breath painfully, "that I shall go away and leave you with That!"

"Leander," said the statue, "command your sister to depart!"

"I'm *not* his"—Matilda was beginning impetuously, till the hairdresser stopped her.

"You *are!*" he cried. "You know you're my sister —you've forgotten it, that's all. . . . Don't say a syllable now, do you hear me? She's going, Lady Venus, going directly!"

"Indeed I'm not," said Matilda, bravely.

"Leave us, maiden!" said the statue. "Your brother is yours no longer, he is mine. Know you who it is that commands? Tremble then, nor oppose the will of Aphrodite of the radiant eyes!"

"I never heard of you before," said Matilda, "but I'm not afraid of you. And, whoever or whatever you are, you shall not take my Leander away against his will. Do you hear? You could never be allowed to do that!"

The statue smiled with pitying scorn. "His own act has given me the power I hold," she said, "and assuredly he shall not escape me!"

"Listen," pleaded Matilda; "perhaps you are not really wicked, it is only that you don't know! The ring he put—without ever thinking what he was doing—on your finger was meant for mine. It was, really! He is my lover; give him back to me!"

"Matilda!" shrieked the wretched man, "you don't know what you're doing. Run away, quick! Do as I tell you!"

"So," said the goddess, turning upon him, "in this, too, you have tried to deceive me! You have loved—you still love this maiden!"

"Oh, not in that way!" he shouted, overcome by his terror for Matilda. "There's some mistake. You mustn't pay any attention to what she says: she's excited. All my sisters get like that when they're excited—they'd say *anything*!"

"Silence!" commanded the statue. "Should not I have skill to read the signs of love? This girl loves you with no sister's love. Deny it not!"

Leander felt that his position was becoming untenable; he could only save Matilda by a partial abandonment. "Well, suppose she does," he said, "I'm not obliged to return it, am I?"

Matilda shrank back. "Oh, Leander!" she cried, with a piteous little moan.

"You've brought it on yourself!" he said; "you will come here interfering!"

"Interfering!" she repeated wildly, "you call it that! How can I help myself? Am I to stand by and see you giving yourself up to, nobody can tell what? As long as I have strength to move and breath to speak I shall stay here, and beg and pray of you not to be so foolish and wicked as to go away with her! How do you know where she will take you to?"

"Cease this railing!" said the statue. "Leander loves you not! Away, then, before I lay you dead at my feet!"

"Leander," cried the poor girl, "tell me: it isn't true what she says? You didn't mean it! you *do* love me! You don't really want me to go away?"

For her own sake he must be cruel; but he could scarcely speak the words that were to drive her from his side for ever. "This—this lady," he said, "speaks quite correct. I—I'd very much rather you went!"

She drew a deep sobbing breath. "I don't care for anything any more!" she said, and faced the statue defiantly. "You say you can strike me dead," she said: "I'm sure I hope you can! And the sooner the better— for I will not leave this room!"

The dreamy smile still curved the statue's lips, in terrible contrast to the inflexible purpose of her next words.

"You have called down your own destruction," she said, "and death shall be yours!"

"Stop a bit," cried Leander, "mind what you're doing! Do you think I'll go with you if you touch a single hair of my poor Tillie's head? Why, I'd sooner stay in prison all my life! See here," and he put his arm round Matilda's slight form; "if you crush her, you crush me—so now!"

"And if so," said the goddess, with cruel contempt, "are you of such value in my sight that I should stay my hand? You, whom I have sought but to manifest my power, for no softer feelings have you ever inspired! And now, having withstood me for so long, you turn, even at the moment of yielding, to yonder creature! And it is enough. I will contend no longer for so mean a prize! Slave and fool that you have shown yourself, Aphrodite rejects you in disdain!"

Leander made no secret of his satisfaction at this. "¡Now you talk sense!" he cried. " I always told you we weren't suited. Tillie, do you hear? She gives me up! She gives me up!"

" Aye," she continued, " I need you not. Upon you and the maiden by your side I invoke a speedy and terrible destruction, which, ere you can attempt to flee, shall surely overtake you!"

Leander was so overcome by this highly unexpected sentence that he lost all control over his limbs; he could only stand where he was, supporting Matilda, and stare at the goddess in fascinated dismay.

The goddess was raising both hands, palm upwards, to the ceiling, and presently she began to chant in a thrilling monotone: " Hear, O Zeus, that sittest on high, delighting in the thunder, hear the prayer of thy daughter, Aphrodite the peerless, as she calleth upon thee, nor suffer her to be set at nought with impunity! Rise now, I beseech thee, and hurl with thine unerring hand a blazing bolt that shall consume these presumptuous insects to a smoking cinder! Blast them, Sire, with the fire-wreaths of thy lightning! blast, and spare not!"

" Kiss me, Tillie, and shut your eyes," said Leander; " it's coming!"

She was nestling close against him, and could not repress a faint shivering moan. " I don't mind, now we're together," she whispered, "if only it won't hurt much!"

The prayer uttered with such deadly intensity had almost ceased to vibrate in their ears, but still the answer tarried; it tarried so long that Leander lost patience, and ventured to open his eyes a little way. He saw the goddess standing there, with a strained expectation on her upturned face.

"I don't wish to hurry you, mum," he said tremulously; "but you ought to be above torturing us. Might I ask you to request your—your relation to look sharp with that thunderbolt?"

"Zeus!" cried the goddess, and her accent was more acute, "thou hast heard—thou wilt not shame me thus! Must I go unavenged?"

Still nothing whatever happened, until at last even Matilda unclosed her eyes. "Leander!" she cried, with a hysterical little laugh, "*I don't believe she can do it!*"

"No more don't I!" said the hairdresser, withdrawing his arm, and coming forward boldly. "Now look here, Lady Venus," he remarked, "it's time there was an end of this, one way or the other; we can't be kept up here all night, waiting till it suits your Mr. Zooce to make cockshies of us. Either let him do it now, or let it alone!"

The statue's face seemed to be illumined by a stronger light. "Zeus, I thank thee!" she exclaimed, clasping her pale hands above her head; "I am answered! I am answered!"

And, as she spoke, a dull ominous rumble was heard in the distance.

"Matilda, here!" cried the terrified hairdresser, running back to his betrothed; "keep close to me. It's all over this time!"

The rumble increased to a roll, which became

"LEANDER!" SHE CRIED, . . . "I DON'T BELIEVE SHE CAN DO IT!"

[*Page* 254

a clanking rattle, and then lessened again to a roll, died away to the original rumble, and was heard no more.

Leander breathed again. "To think of my being taken in like that!" he cried. "Why, it's only a van out in the street! It's no good, mum; you can't work it: you'd better give it up!"

The goddess seemed to feel this herself, for she was wringing her hands with a low wail of despair. "Is there none to hear?" she lamented. "Are they all gone—all? Then is Aphrodite fallen indeed; deserted of the gods, her kinsmen; forgotten of mortals; braved and mocked by such as these! Woe! woe! for Olympus in ruins, and Time the dethroner of deities!"

Leander would hardly have been himself if he had forborne to take advantage of her discomfiture. "You see, mum," he said, "you're not everybody. You mustn't expect to have everything your own way down here. We're in the nineteenth century nowadays, mum, and there's another religion come in since you were the fashion!"

"*Don't*, Leander!" said Matilda, in an undertone; "let her alone, the poor thing!"

She seemed to have quite forgotten that her fallen enemy had been dooming her to destruction the moment before; but there was something so tragic and moving in the sight of such despair that no true woman could be indifferent to it.

Either the taunt or the compassion, however, roused the goddess to a frenzy of passion. "Hold your peace!'' she said fiercely, and strode down upon Leander until he beat an instinctive retreat. "Fallen as I am, I will not brook your mean vauntings or insolent pity! Shorn I may be of my ancient power, but something of my divinity clings to me still. Vengeance is not wholly denied to me! Why should I not deal with you even as with those profane wretches who laid impious hands upon this my effigy? Why? why?"

Leander began to feel uncomfortable again. "If I've said anything you object to," he said hastily, "I'll apologise. I will—and so will Matilda—freely and full; in writing, if that will satisfy you!"

"Tremble not for your worthless bodies," she said; "had you been slain, as I purposed, you would but have escaped me, after all! Now a vengeance keener and more enduring shall be mine! In your gross blindness, you have dared to turn from divine Aphrodite to such a thing as this, and for your impiety you shall suffer! This is your doom, and so much at least I can still accomplish: Long as you both may live, strong as your love may endure, never again shall you see her alone, never more shall she be folded to your breast! For ever, I will stand a barrier between you: so shall your days consume away in the torturing desire for a felicity you may never attain!"

"It seems to me, Tillie," said Leander, looking round at her with hollow eyes, "that we may as well give up keeping company together, after that!"

Matilda had been weeping quietly. "Oh no, Leander, not that! Don't let us give each other up: we may—we may get used to it!"

"That is not all," said the revengeful goddess. "I understand but little of the ways of this degenerate age. But one thing I know: this very night, guards are on their way to search this abode for the image in which I have chosen to reveal myself; and, should they find that they are in search of, you will be dragged to some dungeon, and suffer deserved ignominy. It pleased me yesternight to shield you : to-night, be very sure that this marble form shall not escape their vigilance ! "

He felt at once that this, at least, was no idle threat. The police might arrive at any instant ; she had only to vacate the marble at the moment of their entry—and what could he do ? How could he explain its presence ? The gates of Portland or Dartmoor were already yawning to receive him ! Was it too late, even then, to retrieve the situation ? " If it wasn't for Tillie, I could see my way to something, even now," he thought. " I can but try ! "

" Lady Venus," he began, clearing his throat, " it's not my desire to be the architect of any mutual un-pleasantness—anything but ! I don't see any use in denying that you've got the best of it. I'm done—reg'lar bowled over ; and if ever there was a poor devil of a toad under a harrer, I've no hesitation in admitting that toad's me ! So the only point I should like to submit for your consideration is this : Have things gone too far ? Are you quite sure you won't be spiting yourself as well as me over this business ? Can't we come to an amicable arrangement ? Think it over ! "

" Leander, you can't mean it ! " cried Matilda.

" You leave me alone," he said hoarsely ; " I know what I'm saying ! "

Whether the goddess had overstated her indifference, or whether she may have seen a prospect of some still subtler revenge, she certainly did not receive this proposition of Leander's with the contumely that might have been expected ; on the contrary, she smiled with a triumphant satisfaction that betrayed a disposition to treat.

" Have my words been fulfilled, then ? " she asked. " Is your insolent pride humbled at last ? and do you sue to me for the very favours you so long have spurned?"

"You can put it that way if you like," he said doggedly. "If you want me, you'd better say so while there's time, that's all!"

"Little have you merited such leniency," she said; "and yet, it is to you I owe my return to life and consciousness. Shall I abandon what I have taken such pains to win? No! I accept your submission. Speak, then, the words of surrender, and let us depart together!"

"Before I do that," he said firmly, "there's one point I must have settled to my satisfaction."

"You can bargain still!" she exclaimed haughtily. "Are all barbers like you? If your point concerns the safety of this maiden, be at ease; she shall go unharmed, for she is my rival no longer!"

"Well, it wasn't that exactly," he explained; "but I'm doubtful about that ring being the genuine article, and I want to make sure."

"But a short time since, and you were willing to trust all to me!"

"I was; but, if I may take the liberty of observing so, things were different then. You were wrong about that thunderbolt—you may be wrong about the ring!"

"Fool!" she said, "how know you that the quality of the token concerns my power? Were it even of unworthy metal, has it not brought me hither?"

"Yes," he said, "but it mightn't be strong enough to pass *me* the whole distance, and where should I be then? It don't look more to me than 15 carat, and I daren't run any extra risk."

"How, then, can your doubts be set at rest?" she demanded.

"Easy," he replied: "there are men who understand

these things. All I ask of you is to step over with me, and see one of them, and take his opinion; and if he says it's gold—why, then I shall know where I am!"

"Aphrodite submit her claims to the judgment of a mortal!" she cried. "Never will I thus debase myself!"

"Very well," he said, "then we must stay where we are. All I can say is, I've made you a fair offer."

She paused. "Why not?" she said dreamily, as if thinking aloud. "Have not I sued ere this for the decision of a shepherd judge—even of Paris? 'Tis but one last indignity, and then—he is mine indeed! Leander," she added graciously, "it shall be as you will. Lead the way; I follow!"

But Matilda, who had been listening to this compromise with incredulous horror, clung in desperation to her lover's arm, and sought to impede his flight. "Leander!" she cried, "oh, Leander! surely you won't be mad enough to go away with her! You won't be so wicked and sinful as that! Remember who she is: one of the false gods of the poor benighted heathens—she owned it herself! She's nothing less than a live idol! Think of all the times we've been to chapel together; think of your dear aunt, and how she'll feel your being in such awful company! Let the police come, and think what they like: we'll tell them the truth, and make them believe it. Only be brave, and stay here with me; don't let her ensnare you! Have some pity for me; for, if you leave me, I shall die!"

"Already the guards are at your gates," said the statue; "choose quickly—while you may!"

He put Matilda gently from him: "Tillie," he said, with a convulsive effort to remain calm, "you gave me up of your own free will—you know that—and now you've come round too late. The other lady spoke first!"

As she still clung to him, he tried to whisper some last words of a consoling or reassuring nature, and she suddenly relaxed her grasp, and allowed him to make his escape without further dissuasion—not that his arguments had reconciled her to his departure, but because she was mercifully unaware of it.

THE ODD TRICK

XV.

> "O heart of stone, are you flesh, and caught
>   By that you swore to withstand?"
>
> Maud.

OUTSIDE on the stairs Leander suddenly remembered that his purpose might be as far as ever from being accomplished. The house was being watched : to be seen leaving it would procure his instant arrest.

Hastily excusing himself to the goddess, he rushed down to his laboratory, where he knew there was a magnificent beard and moustache which he had been constructing for some amateur theatricals. With these, and a soft felt hat, he completed a disguise in which he flattered himself he was unrecognisable.

The goddess, however, penetrated it as soon as he rejoined her. "Why have you thus transformed your-self?" she inquired coldly.

"Because," explained Leander, "seeing the police are all on the look-out for me, I thought it couldn't do any harm."

"It is useless !" she returned.

"To be sure," he agreed blankly, " they'll expect me to go out disguised. If only they aren't up to the way out by the back ! That's our only chance now."

"Leave all to me," she replied calmly ; " with Aphrodite you are safe."

And he never did quite understand how that strange elopement was effected, or even remember whether they left the house from the front or rear. The statue glided swiftly on, and, grasping a corner of her robe, he followed, with only the vaguest sense of obstacles overcome and passed as in a dream.

By the time he had completely regained his senses he was in a crowded thoroughfare, which he recognised as the Gray's Inn Road.

A certain scheme from which, desperate as it was, he hoped much, might be executed as well here as elsewhere, and he looked about him for the aid on which he counted.

"Where, then, lives the wise man whom you would consult?" said Aphrodite.

Leander went on until he could see the coloured lights of a chemist's window, and then he said, "There—right opposite!"

He felt strangely nervous himself, but the goddess seemed even more so. She hung back all at once, and clutched his arm in her marble grasp.

"Leander," she said, "I will not go! See those liquid fires glowing in lurid hues, like the eyes of some dread monster! This test of yours is needless, and I fear it."

"Lady Venus," he said earnestly, "I do assure you they're only big bottles, and quite harmless too, having water in them, not physic. You've no call to be alarmed."

She yielded, and they crossed the road. The shop was small and unpretending. In the window the chief ornaments were speckled plaster limbs clad in elastic socks, and photographs of hideous complaints before and after treatment with a celebrated ointment; and there were certain trophies which indicated that the chemist numbered dentistry among his accomplishments.

Inside, the odour of drugs prevailed, in the absence of the subtle perfume that is part of the fittings of a fashionable apothecary, and on the very threshold the goddess paused irresolute.

"'There is magic in the air," she exclaimed, "and fearful poisons. This man is some enchanter!"

"Now I put it to you," said Leander, with some impatience, "does he *look* it?"

The chemist was a mild little man, with a high forehead, round spectacles, a little red beak of a nose, and a weak grey beard. As they entered, he was addressing a small and draggled child from behind his counter. "Go back and tell your mother," he said, "that she must come herself. I never sell paregoric to children."

There was so little of the wizard in his manner that the goddess, who possibly had some reason to mistrust a mortal magician, was reassured.

As the child retired, the chemist turned to them with a look of bland and dignified inquiry (something, perhaps the consciousness of having once passed an examination, sustains the meekest chemist in an inward superiority). He did not speak.

Leander took it upon himself to explain. "This lady would be glad to be told whether a ring she's got on is the real article or only imitation," he said, "so she thought you could decide it for her."

"Not so," corrected the goddess, austerely. "For myself I care not!"

"Have it your own way!" said Leander. "*I* should like to be told, then. I suppose, mister, you've some way of testing these things?"

"Oh yes," said the chemist; "I can treat it for you

with what we call *aquafortis*, a combination of nitric and hydrochloric acid, which would tell us at once. I ought to mention, perhaps, that so extremely powerful an agent may injure the appearance of the metal if it is of inferior quality. Will the lady oblige me with the ring?"

Aphrodite extended her hand with haughty indifference. The chemist examined the ring as it circled her finger, and Leander held his breath in tortures of anxiety. A horrible fear came over him that his deep-laid scheme was about to end in failure.

But the chemist remarked at last: "Exactly; thank you, madam. The gold is antique, certainly; but I should be inclined to pronounce it, at first sight, genuine. I will ascertain how this is, if you will take the trouble to remove the ring and pass it over!"

"Why?" demanded Aphrodite, obstinately.

"I could not undertake to treat it while it remains upon your hand," he protested. "The acid might do some injury!"

"It matters not!" she said calmly; and Leander recollected with horror that, as any injury to her statue would have no physical effect upon the goddess herself, she could not be much influenced by the chemist's reason.

"Do what the gentleman tells you," he said, in an eager whisper, as he drew her aside.

"I know your wiles, O perfidious one," she said. "Having induced me to remove this token, you would seize it yourself, and take to flight! I will not remove this ring!"

"There's a thing to say!" said Leander; "there's a suspicion to throw against a man! If you think I'm likely to do that, I'll go right over here, where I can't even see it, and I won't stir out till it's all over. Will that satisfy you? You know why I'm so anxious about that ring; and now, when the gentleman tells you he's almost sure it's gold—— "

" It *is* gold!" said the goddess.

" If you're so sure about it," he retaliated, " why are you afraid to have it proved?"

" I am not afraid," she said; "but I require no proof!"

" I do," he retorted, "and what I told you before I stand to. If that ring is proved—in the only way it can be proved, I mean, by this gentleman testing it as he tells you he can—then there's no more to be said, and I'll go away with you like a lamb. But without that proof I won't stir a step, and so I tell you. It won't take a moment. You can see for yourself that I couldn't possibly catch up the ring from here!"

" Swear to me," she said, " that you will remain where you now stand; and remember," she added, with an accent of triumph, " our compact is that, should yonder man pronounce that the ring has passed through the test with honour, you will follow me whithersoever I bid you!"

" You have only to lead the way," he said, "and I promise you faithfully I'll follow."

Goddesses may be credited with some knowledge of the precious metals, and Aphrodite had no doubt of the result of the chemist's investigations. So it was with an air of serene anticipation that she left Leander upon this, and advanced to the chemist's counter.

" Prove it now," she said, "quickly, that I may go!"

The chemist, who had been waiting in considerable bewilderment, prepared himself to receive the ring, and Leander, keeping his distance, felt his heart beating fast as Aphrodite slowly drew the token from her finger, and placed it in the chemist's outstretched hand.

Scarcely had she done so, as the chemist was retiring with the ring to one of his lamps, before the goddess seemed suddenly aware that she had committed a fatal error.

She made a stride forward to follow and recover it; but, as if some unseen force was restraining her, she stopped short, and a rush of whirling words, in some tongue unknown both to Leander and the chemist, forced its way through lips that smiled still, though they were freezing fast.

Then, with a strange hoarse cry of baffled desire and revenge, she succeeded, by a violent effort, in turning, and bore down with tremendous force upon the cowering hairdresser, who gave himself up at once for lost.

But the marble was already incapable of obeying her will. Within a few paces from him the statue stopped for the last time, with an abruptness that left it quivering and rocking. A greyish hue came over the face, causing the borrowed tints to stand forth, crude and glaring; the arms waved wildly and impotently once or twice, and then grew still for ever, in the attitude conceived long since by the Grecian sculptor!

Leander was free! His hazardous experiment had succeeded. As it was the ring which had brought the passionate, imperious goddess into her marble counterfeit, so—the ring once withdrawn—her power was instantly at an end, and the spell which had enabled her to assume a form of stone was broken.

He had hoped for this, had counted upon it, but even yet hardly dared to believe in his deliverance.

He had not done with it yet, however; for he would have to get the statue out of that shop, and abandon it in some manner which would not compromise himself, and it is by no means an easy matter to mislay a life-size and invaluable antique without attracting an inconvenient amount of attention.

The chemist, who had been staring meanwhile in blank astonishment, now looked inquiringly at Leander, who looked helplessly at him.

At last the latter, unable to be silent any longer, said, " The lady seems unwell, sir."

" Why," Leander admitted, " she does appear a little out of sorts."

" Has she had these attacks before, do you happen to know ? "

" She's more often like this than not," said Leander.

" Dear me, sir; but that's very serious. Is there nothing that gives relief?—a little sal volatile, now? Does the lady carry smelling salts? If not, I could——" And the chemist made an offer to come from behind his counter to examine the strange patient.

" No," said Leander, hastily. " Don't you trouble—you leave her to me. I know how to manage her. When she's rigid like this, she can't bear to be taken notice of."

He was wondering all the time how he was to get away with her, until the chemist, who seemed at least as anxious for her departure, suggested the answer: " I should imagine the poor lady would be best at home. Shall I send out for a cab ? " he asked.

" Yes," said Leander, gratefully ; " bring a hansom. She'll come round better in the open air ; " for he had his doubts whether the statue could be stowed inside a four-wheeler.

" I'll go myself," said the obliging man ; " my assistant's out. Perhaps the lady will sit down till the cab comes ? "

"Thanks," said Leander; "but when she's like this, she's been recommended to stand."

The chemist ran out bare-headed, to return presently with a cab and a small train of interested observers. He offered the statue his arm to the cab-door, an attention which was naturally ignored.

"We shall have to carry her there," said Leander.

"Why, bless me, sir," said the chemist, as he helped to lift her, "she—she's surprisingly heavy!"

"Yes," gasped Leander, over her unconscious shoulder; "when she goes off in one of these sleeps, she does sleep very heavy"—an explanation which, if obscure, was accepted by the other as part of the general strangeness of the case.

On the threshold the chemist stopped again. "I'd almost forgotten the ring," he said.

"*I'll* take that!" said Leander.

"Excuse me," was the objection, "but I was to give it back to the lady herself. Had I not better put it on her finger, don't you think?"

"Are you a married man?" asked Leander, grimly.

"Yes," said the chemist.

"Then, if you'll take my advice, I wouldn't if I was you—if you're at all anxious to keep out of trouble. You'd better give the ring to me, and I give you my word of honour as a gentleman that I'll give it back to her as soon as ever she's well enough to ask for it."

The other adopted the advice, and, amidst the sympathy of the bystanders, they got the statue into the cab.

"Where to?" asked the man through the trap.

"Charing Cross," said Leander, at random; he ought the drive would give him time for reflection.

"The 'orspital, eh?" said the cabman, and drove off,

leaving the mild chemist to stare open-mouthed on the pavement for a moment, and go back to his shop with a growing sense that he had had a very unusual experience.

Now that Leander was alone in the cab with the statue, whose attitude required space, and cramped him uncomfortably, he wondered more and more what he was to do with it. He could not afford to drive about London for ever with her; he dared not take her home; and he was afraid of being seen with her!

All at once he seemed to see a way out of his difficulty. His first step was to do what he could, in the constantly varying light, to reduce the statue to its normal state. He removed the curls which had disfigured her classical brow, and, with his pocket-handkerchief, rubbed most of the colour from her face; then the cloak had only to be torn off, and all that could betray him was gone.

Near Charing Cross, Leander told the driver to take him down Parliament Street, and stop at the entrance to Scotland Yard; there the cabman, at Leander's request, descended, and stared to find him huddled up under the gleaming pale arms of a statue.

"Guv'nor," he remarked, "that warn't the fare I took up, I'll take my dying oath!"

"It's all right," said Leander. "Now, I tell you what I want you to do: go straight in through the archway, find a policeman, and say there's a gentleman in your cab that's found a valuable article that's been missing, and wants assistance in bringing it in. I'll take care of the cab, and here's double fare for your trouble."

"And wuth it, too," was the cabman's comment, as he departed on his mission. "I thought it was the devil I was a drivin', we was that down on the orfside !"

It was no part of Leander's programme to wait for his return ; he threw the cloak over his arm, pocketed his beard, and slipped out of the cab and across the road to a spot whence he could watch unseen. And when he had seen the cabman come with two constables, he felt assured that his burden was in safe hands at last, and returned to Southampton Row as quickly as the next hansom he hailed could take him.

He entered his house by the back entrance : it was unguarded ; and although he listened long at the foot of the stairs, he heard nothing. Had the Inspector not come yet, or was there a trap? As he went on, he fancied there were sounds in his sitting-room, and went up to the door and listened nervously before entering in.

"Oh, Miss Collum, my poor dear !" a tremulous voice, which he recognised as his aunt's, was saying, "for Mercy's sake, don't lie there like that ! She's dying !—and it's my fault for letting her come here !—and what am I to say to her ma ? "

Leander had heard enough ; he burst in, with a white, horror-stricken face. Yes, it was too true ! Matilda was lying back in his crazy armchair, her eyes fast closed, her lips parted.

"Aunt," he said with difficulty, "she's not—not *dead ?* "

"If she is not," returned his aunt, "it's no thanks to you, Leandy Tweddle ! Go away ; you can do no good to her now !"

"Not till I've heard her speak," cried Tweddle. "Tillie, don't you hear ?—it's me ! "

To his immense relief, she opened her eyes at the

HE THREW HIMSELF DOWN BY HER CHAIR, AND DREW DOWN THE
HANDS IN WHICH SHE HAD HIDDEN HER FACE.

[*Page* 277.

sound of his voice, and turned away with a feeble gesture of fear and avoidance. " You have come back ! " she moaned, " and with her ! Oh, keep her away ! . . . I can't bear it all over again ! . . . I can't ! "

He threw himself down by her chair, and drew down the hands in which she had hidden her face. " Matilda, my poor, hardly-used darling ! " he said, " I've come back *alone !* I've got rid of her, Tillie ! I'm free ; and there's no one to stand between us any more ! "

She pushed back her disordered fair hair, and looked at him with sweet, troubled eyes. " But you went away with her—for ever ? " she said. " You said you didn't love me any longer. I heard you . . . it was just before——" and she shuddered at the recollection.

" I know," said Leander, soothingly. " I was obligated to speak harsh, to deceive the—the other party, Tillie. I tried to tell you, quiet-like, that you wasn't to mind ; but you wouldn't take no notice. But there, we won't talk about it any more, so long as you forgive me ; and you do, don't you ? "

She hid her face against his shoulder, in answer, from which he drew a favourable conclusion ; but Miss Tweddle was not so easily pacified.

" And is this all the explanation you're going to give," she demanded, " for treating this poor child the way you've done, and neglecting her shameful like this ? If she's satisfied, Leandy, I'm not."

" I can't help it, aunt," he said. I've been true to Tillie all the way through, in spite of all appearances to the contrary—as she knows now. And the more I explained, the less you'd understand about it ; so we'll leave things where they are. But I've got back the ring, and now you shall see me put it on her finger."

* * * * * *

It seemed that Leander had driven to Scotland Yard just in time to save himself, for the Inspector did not make his threatened search that evening.

Two or three days later, however, to Leander's secret alarm, he entered the shop. After all, he felt, it was hopeless to think of deceiving these sleuth-hounds of the Law: this detective had been making inquiries, and identified him as the man who had shared the hansom with that statue !

His knees trembled as he stood behind his glass-topped counter. "Come to make the search, sir?" he said, as cheerfully as he could. "You'll find us ready for you."

"Well," said Inspector Bilbow, with a queer mixture of awkwardness and complacency, "no, not exactly. Tweddle, my good fellow, circumstances have recently assumed a shape that renders a search unnecessary, as perhaps you are aware?"

He looked very hard at Tweddle as he spoke, and the hairdresser felt that this was a crucial moment—the detective was still uncertain whether he had been mixed up with the affair or not. Leander's faculty of ready wit served him better here than on past occasions.

"Aware? No, sir!" he said, with admirable simplicity. "Then that's why you didn't come the other evening ! I sat up for you, sir; all night I sat up."

"The fact of the matter is, Tweddle," said Bilbow, who had become suddenly affable and condescending, "I found myself reduced, so to speak, to make use of you as a false clue, if you catch my meaning?"

"I can't say I do quite understand, sir."

"I mean—of course, I saw with half an eye, bless your soul, that you'd had nothing to do with it— it wasn't likely that a poor chap like you had any knowledge of a big plant of that description. No, no; don't you go away with that idea. I never associated you with it for a single instant."

"I'm truly glad to hear it, Mr. Inspector," said Leander.

"It was owing to the line I took up. There were the real parties to put off their guard, and to do that, Tweddle—to do that, it was necessary to appear to suspect you. D'ye see?"

"I think it was a little hard on me, sir," he said; "for being suspected like that hurts a man's feelings, sir. I did feel wounded to have that cast up against me!"

"Well, well," said the Inspector, "we'll go into that later. But, to go on with what I was saying. My tactics, Tweddle, have been crowned with success—the famous Venus is now safe in my hands! What do you say to that?"

"Say? Why, what clever gentlemen you detective officers are, to be sure!" cried Leander.

"Well, to be candid, there's not many in the Department that would have managed the job as neatly; but, then, it was a case I'd gone into, and thoroughly got up."

"That I'm sure you must have done, sir," agreed Leander. "How ever did you come on it?" He felt a kind of curiosity to hear the answer.

"Tweddle," was the solemn reply, "that is a thing you must be content to leave in its native mystery" (which Leander undoubtedly was). "We in the Criminal Investigation Department have our secret channels and our underground sources for obtaining information, but to lay those channels and sources bare to the public would serve no useful end, nor would it be an expedient act on my part. All you have any claim to be told is, that, however costly and complicated, however dangerous even, the means employed may have been (that I say nothing about), the ultimate end has been obtained. The Venus, sir, will be restored to her place in the Gallery at Wricklesmarsh Court, without a scratch on her!"

"You don't say so! Lor!" cried Leander, hoping that his countenance would keep his secret, "well, there now! And my ring, sir, if you remember—isn't *that* on her?"

"You mustn't expect us to do everything. Your ring was, as I had every reason to expect it would be, missing. But I shall be talking the matter over with Sir Peter Purbecke, who's just come back to Wricklesmarsh from the Continent, and, provided—ahem!—you don't go talking about this affair, I should feel justified in recommending him to make you some substantial acknowledgment for any—well, little inconvenience you may have been put to on account of your slight connection with the business, and the steps I may have thought proper to take in consequence. And, from all I hear of Sir Peter, I think he would be inclined to come down uncommonly handsome."

"Well, Mr. Inspector," said Leander, "all I can say is this: if Sir Peter was to know the life his statue has led me for the past few days, I think he'd say I deserved it—I do, indeed!"

*　　*　　*　　*　　*　　*

CONCLUSION.

The narrow passage off Southampton Row is at present without a hairdresser's establishment, Leander having resigned his shop, long since, in favour of either a fruiterer or a stationer.

But, in one of the leading West End thoroughfares there is a large and prosperous haircutting saloon, over which the name of "Tweddle" glitters resplendent, and the books of which would prove too much for Matilda, even if more domestic duties had not begun to claim her attention.

Leander's troubles are at end. Thanks to Sir Peter Purbecke's munificence, he has made a fresh start; and, so far, Fortune has prospered him. The devices he has invented for correcting Nature's more palpable errors in taste are becoming widely known, while he is famous, too, as the gifted author of a series of brilliant and popular hairwashes. He is accustoming his clients to address him as "Professor"—a title which he has actually had conferred upon him from a quarter in which he is, perhaps, the most highly appreciated—for prosperity has not exactly lessened his self-esteem.

Mr. Jauncy, too, is a married man, although he does not respond so heartily to congratulations. There is no intimacy between the two households, the heads of which recognise that, as Leander puts it, "their wives harmonise better apart."

To the new collection of Casts from the Antique, at South Kensington, there has been recently added one which appears in the official catalogue under the following description :—

"*The Cytherean Venus.*—Marble statue. Found in a grotto in the Island of Cerigo. Now in the collection of Sir Peter Purbecke, at Wricklesmarsh Court, Blackheath.

"This noble work has been indifferently assigned to various periods; the most general opinion, however, pronounces it to be a copy of an earlier work of Alkamenes, or possibly Kephisodotos.

THE TINTED VENUS.

"The unusual smallness of the extremities seems to betray the hand of a restorer, and there are traces of colour in the original marble, which are supposed to have been added at a somewhat later period."

Should Professor Tweddle ever find himself in the Museum on a Bank Holiday, and enter the new gallery, he could hardly avoid seeing the magnificent cast numbered 333 in the catalogue, and reviving thereby recollections he has almost succeeded in suppressing.

But this is an experience he will probably spare himself; for he is known to entertain, on principle, very strong prejudices against sculpture, and more particularly the Antique.

THE END.

LONDON: PRINTED BY WILLIAM CLOWES AND SONS, LIMITED,
STAMFORD STREET AND CHARING CROSS.